COMING OF AGE DAY

PRESENTED BY:

KAIJU ASSAULT

by Dane G. Kroll

cover art by

Travis Molitor

interior art by

Tanner Wright

Books by Dane G. Kroll

All Ages

Greg and Lucy's Hole World

Kaiju Series

Realm of Goryo: The Four Pillars
Realm of Goryo: The Culling
Realm of Goryo: The Riven Mother
Realm of Goryo: Baptism
Realm of Goryo: Arms Race
Realm of Goryo: Kaiju in the Machine

Sci-Fi/Adventure

Lariat Rhodes and the Perils of the Fantasy Stars

Fantasy

Eluan Falls: The Inheritors of the World
Eluan Falls: The Tides of Utter Undoing
Eluan Falls: A Whisper of Fate

Horror

Psalm Springs
Black Friday
We Woke the Dead

Dedicated to
Lara

Thanks for spending
life with me

Additional thanks:
The Kaiju Assault Team
Brandon Phillips, Jack Armstrong,
and Alan Berckenoff

KAIJU ASSAULT PRESENTS:

COMING OF AGE DAY

kaijuassault.com

Chapter 1

Violent thunder rolled through the streets of Tokyo on a clear sunny day. A shadow cast down onto thousands of people evacuating the city. The trains were filled to the brim with passengers. Cars were stationary, nose to nose, on the highway. All in an effort to escape the destructive path of the kaiju, Matamerra.

Matamerra paused for a moment in the heart of Tokyo. Its fatty blue body jostled as the kaiju absorbed an attack of artillery from the Kaiju Assault Research and Retaliation Division of the Japanese Armed Forces; more popularly known as K.A.R.R.D. Unfortunately, Matamerra's shell allowed the kaiju to shrug off the pain and contemplate its next move.

First, Matamerra turned its attention to the soldiers on the ground. Bolt tanks littered the streets, destroying cars in the process, to get close to the kaiju.

Soldiers hurriedly rushed people out of harm's way. But it was too late. Matamerra arched back, sticking out its stomach and the orifice at the center of its body. Frostfire shot out of Matamerra.

The beam sliced across several K.A.R.R.D. vehicles and soldiers, freezing everything it touched. A blizzard of ice cascaded through the streets. The last moments of people's lives were frozen in time, fear stuck on their face until thawed.

Matamerra patted its belly with cherished victory. It's small trunk lifted into the air. A new scent caught the kaiju's attention and Matamerra shifted its body to the right. The kaiju screeched out of its beak for the entire city to hear. Matamerra was on the move once again.

The Keiro Gardens Retirement Home was no longer the peaceful final home for its residents and families. A line of buses was parked outside of the complex, piling in as many people as they could. Matamerra's presence in Tokyo already set an evacuation in order but its newest trajectory put the retirement home directly in the kaiju's path.

Senior Police Officer Ishida Katashi of the Tokyo Metropolitan Police Department stood in the center of the lobby gesturing with wide arms for the people inside to keep moving. It was his responsibility to ensure all of the residents were safely evacuated from the area before Matamerra arrived.

From the corner of his eye, Katashi could see the blue blurry image of the kaiju in the distance. They were cutting it close. In a few minutes the building would be within range of its frostfire. He couldn't rush the older residents much more, and truth be told the addition of families trying to help get their older relatives out of the building was not helping. It was only adding to the congestion.

"Only one family member inside at a time!" Katashi ordered to deaf ears. "We don't need more people inside than out!"

The building rumbled as if angry itself at Katashi's poor management of the situation. He lamented that it had gotten so out of hand. But the love for a family member would drive anybody crazy.

Down the hall, amidst the confusion, Nakada Himari was being cared for her by her son and his family of four. Himari sat in a rocking chair with a shawl across her lap. Her ninety-four year old body did not want to get up until she had to. Her son, Toshiaki, paced from one end to the other. Every time the building rumbled he would stop and grab his heart. Under his breath, Himari could hear him grumble about the location of the retirement home, wishing he had chosen the more expensive one outside of the city.

At Himari's side, her grandson, Keiichi, rolled his eyes. He was pretending to play it cool, but Himari could see the teenager's apprehension. Himari reached over and grabbed her grandson's hand.

"Hold my hand," she said to Keiichi. "I'm scared."

Keiichi didn't hesitate. He grasped his grandmother's frail hand, wanting to be the strength to get her through this event.

Near the door, Himari's other grandchild, Emi, stood quiet. Her young mind didn't comprehend what was truly going on, but she could sense the fear that was spreading around her. She whimpered every time there was a rumble.

"That's it. We have to go," said Aika, pulling her husband away from packing anymore knick knacks into the suitcase.

"But the pictures," argued Toshiaki.

"We can come back for them," assured Aika. She gave her husband a gentle kiss.

As the parents spoke, Emi's eyes wandered to the room

across the hall. She read the name, slowly in her head, posted on the door: *Room 14, Stan*. People rushed past her through the halls, blurring her vision, but one constant was homed in on.

An old man sat alone in the room. He sat on a chair looking out the window. The tray of food by his side was untouched.

Emi stepped across the hall, dodging evacuating residents. She stepped into the quiet room, glad to have a moment of peace. The young girl stared at the older gentleman. His clothes were ragged and musty. Emi stopped just inside the doorway.

Pictures of a young woman were placed in various spots of the small room. Several pictures of a happy family were knocked over. The ones that remained standing danced on the surface of cabinets every time Matamerra took a step across the city.

"Are you leaving?" Emi asked.

The old man didn't respond.

"Where's your family?"

Then the old man grumbled.

"There's a monster coming," said Emi.

The old man turned his head. He glanced down at the young girl. Then up at the family across the hall. Himari was being helped to her feet by her son and daughter-in-law.

"Maybe you can come with us?!" Emi announced with a smile. Then she heard the rustling of her family on their feet. She turned away from the old man she was talking to and returned to the room across the hall.

"Emi! Don't walk away like that!" her mother scolded her.

"Take my hand. We have to go."

"But what about-" Emi said before her mother cut her off.

The old man's blank stare turned toward the family across the hall. Himari was going to be saved by her family. A family that loved her. That cherished their elders.

The old man got to his feet. His hand brushed across his tray of food. His fingers danced across his plate until his fingertips wrapped around the handle of the knife he was given.

He proceeded to walk across the hall to the family failing to escape harm's way. Their screams drowned out by the chaos of the oncoming kaiju.

The rumbles of Matamerra grew stronger. But Ishida Katashi was growing more confident. The lobby was finally looking clear. Only a handful of buses remained outside in the parking lot.

The kaiju was several blocks away. Katashi left his post at the main lobby and began to do a final sweep of the area. He checked one room after the other. Every few seconds Matamerra's footsteps lasted longer and did more damage. Every so often, Katashi could feel the reverberation of the kaiju's frostfire hit a nearby building. Katashi prayed with every blast that it would not be the one that took him out.

After making his rounds through the complex, Katashi made his final pass of a hallway that would lead him back to the lobby and off to safety. The building was evacuated. Against all odds, Katashi had done it.

At least that's what he thought.

A scream from down the hall echoed in his ear. Katashi looked forward. The head nurse, Kawahara Kyo, collapsed along the wall of the hallway. Katashi rushed forward to join her. The older woman's screaming didn't stop as she pointed into one of the rooms.

Katashi approached the door that Kyo was pointing at. Katashi rushed in. And for a moment, the danger of Matamerra nearby was overshadowed by the graceful touch of death itself.

Dead bodies were strewn about. Blood splattered across the walls and the ceilings.

Keiichi's body was half under the bed. His legs were shredded in a pool of blood. Toshiaki and Aika were on the floor. Their backs covered in blood.

Finally, Katashi's eyes settled on Himari's rocking chair. Two bloody wounds stained her blanket and blouse. Emi was in her arms.

The little girl reached out. She was still alive.

Katashi stepped back. The scene was fresh. Blood was still seeping out of the bodies. He shook his head unable to comprehend what he was looking at.

Kyo's screams continued. Demanding answers from the horrific scene.

Katashi tried to clear his head, but Matamerra's presence only complicated the matter. The building rumbled. Dust and debris sprinkled down from the ceiling. It would not be long before the building was destroyed.

Katashi turned around to look back at Kyo, but his attention was drawn into the room across the hall.

He looked directly into the eyes of the old man back in his rocking chair. He stared back at Katashi with a smile. The bloody knife still in his hands.

"No," said Katashi. "No, no, no..."

Katashi's refusal of reality was overpowered by the sound of Matamerra approaching the area. The ground shook, throwing Katashi off his feet.

The old man's smile opened. A dark laugh roared out of the small room of his.

Kyo scrambled. The head nurse needed to escape.

She rushed up to Katashi. Her fingers clawed at the police officer, demanding a safe retreat. Katashi brushed her off. He stepped forward back toward the murder scene and the little girl that was reaching out for help.

Then the ceiling of Keiro Gardens collapsed. Chunks of cement and metal fell onto Katashi, Kyo, and the rooms around them.

It was too late.

Katashi had hesitated.

Stan began to laugh.

Kyo's desperate plea to escape overpowered any other of

Katashi's decisions. He could save at least one he told himself.

The police officer grabbed hold of Kyo and ran away from the murder scene. Despite the roaring of Matamerra just over his head, Katashi could still hear the sound of the old man's laughter.

Katashi rushed out of the retirement complex with the head nurse. A lone car waited in an empty parking lot. He looked up to see Matamerra directly overhead. The blue skinned kaiju stepped forward.

A massive foot came crashing down onto the building Katashi was just occupying. He was brought to his knees. Dirt and debris blew past him. Kyo collapsed onto the pavement, feint with exhaustion.

Matamerra did not stop. The kaiju kept moving forward. The retirement complex wasn't even a second thought.

Katashi remained on the pavement. He feared even breathing would lure the kaiju back. He stared out at Matamerra for a moment, but his attention was pulled back toward the retirement home.

Where once stood a peaceful building, was now a broken lot. The destruction would forever hold its secrets and grip onto the deaths that it saw in its final moments.

And there was nothing Katashi could do about it.

Chapter 2

15 years later

January 15- Coming of Age Day

A rustic sign displayed proudly the beauty of Gracefields Cemetery. The sun was setting on the mid-January day. A light snow blanketed the gravestones. The caretaker, Yukio, peddled a small bike through the grounds. He dismissed several pieces of litter on his way back to the main office. His entire reputation was a sham. Gracefields Cemetery got its beauty more so from the families of loved ones buried there more so than Yukio himself.

Yukio was hunched over the handlebar on his bike. He teetered on the verge of collapse. One tipsy move of the head could send him crashing down at the end of the day. The suit he wore looked nice from a glance, but as the details emerged it was clear just how rundown his clothes were. Often times Yukio would build his wardrobe from clothes left over from a body's fitting at the adjacent funeral home. Most of the time, the family simply forgot about the other suits or didn't bother to collect them. Every once in a while Yukio would find something he really liked and nab it without anybody noticing.

His final duty of the day was to make sure the grounds were clear and to lock up. There were still a few more hours in the day but with the sun setting early the cemetery rarely had visitors that late. Yukio was going to take that advantage and get home as soon as possible.

Up ahead, Yukio spied a young couple. The last two visitors to the cemetery stood together at a gravestone. The young man held his head low. His girlfriend had one arm wrapped around his waist. Yukio could hear soft crying as he made his approach.

"We're closing up," he said without warning.

The couple didn't hear him at first.

"I said we're closing up," said Yukio, riding his bike next to the two visitors. In order to get their attention Yukio came up between the couple and the gravestone. The front wheel of his bike was encroaching on the surface of the gravesite.

"Time to move on," said Yukio.

The young man burst out into harsher tears. He couldn't form the words to talk back to Yukio.

"You can come back tomorrow," said Yukio. "But you gotta go."

Speechless from her disgust, the woman grabbed a hold of her boyfriend and gently ushered him away. Yukio was two steps behind them, scooting his bike forward. He would escort them out of the cemetery step by step if he had to.

Yukio watched the couple get into their car and drive away. He smiled as the last of his visitors were gone. He could lock up with ease now.

Then a rustle came from the trees nearby.

Yukio looked over. He didn't see anything in the shadows of

the bushes. The sound came from a part of the cemetery that didn't get much attention. Its landscaping was overrun with weeds. The pathway to that section of the cemetery was covered with overgrowth. Yukio told his bosses he would get to that section, but it was never a high priority. That part of the cemetery was for the lost and forgotten. People that died with no family, even no names, were laid to rest there. Nobody ever came to visit. Thus, nobody ever complained that the area was a mess.

"Dang, kids," said Yukio.

The only visitors that section of the cemetery had were teenagers looking to hook up. Yukio took joy in interrupting the carnal heat that could be found there. They would scramble for their clothes while Yukio laughed and got a good peek at the young girls.

The rustling in the bushes continued. Yukio shook his head as he put his bike down. He would have to enter by foot.

The cold air whisked around his face. Yukio adjusted his stalking cap, giving a boost of warmth to his ears. He walked forward, investigating the source of the sound. It was probably a squirrel, but a new warmth in his groin said it was something better.

Yukio stepped quietly through the weeds. He wanted to sneak up on his targets. If he spooked them too early, he wouldn't get to see the show.

Leaves rustled just up ahead. Yukio hunched low. He could see several bushes near a cluster of grave markers move. It was just a few feet ahead of him.

Yukio smiled then he jumped forward, out into the open.

"Fun's over!" he yelled.

But no one was there.

Yukio froze with disappointment, one hand pointing in the direction of the exit, the other absentmindedly rubbing his crotch.

"Blasted raccoons," Yukio swore.

He turned around to return to his bike. He wanted to get home faster than ever.

Suddenly, a shadow struck out from the trees.

A sharp pain cut into Yukio's groin. A boney spike ripped upward through the groundskeeper's body, catching his hand as well.

Yukio screamed in agony.

Then a second spike swung out directly at Yukio's face. The boney spike plunged into Yukio's screaming mouth and ripped through the back of the head.

His scream was muffled as blood poured out of every orifice. Then it was replaced with the final gags of death.

The winter night went silent.

Yuki's head slid off the boney spike, leaving a trail of blood.

His body collapsed onto the snowy ground. More blood stained the white serene moment in time.

Heavy footsteps crunched along the snow and weeds. The war drums marched from the land of the dead. A hymn for the youth to dread.

Chapter 3

The community that once housed the Keiro Gardens Retirement Home was now a completely new part of town. Apartment complexes stood where small shops and the retirement home itself once were. Small rooms stacked on one another, cramming as many families as it could inside. The destruction from Matamerra was a developer's dream.

The folks that once lived in Keiro Gardens and survived Matamerra's onslaught were left homeless in the aftermath. The new developers did not care. They wanted a better avenue for money: the young up and coming family.

The former residents were forced to move back in with their families if they couldn't find another place to live right away. Some families welcomed the edition with open arms. Others were less fortunate.

Soon Keiro Gardens was nothing but an afterthought for the Rising Peaks apartment building, and the families that made a home there.

Ota Masaki brushed her hair in the mirror of her bedroom on the seventeenth floor. The morning light filled her tiny space and reflected off her black hair. She wore a furisode, a ceremonial kimono, red with gold decretive lace. It was to mark the special occasion of turning twenty that year. Masaki's birthday wasn't until July but Coming of Age Day was the day everybody celebrated. It was great because Masaki and many of her friends were all celebrating together. It was something they had been looking forward to for several years.

Behind her, Hatanaka Eri, Masaki's best friend, was sprawled out on Masaki's bed. Her kimono was less high end than Masaki's. She wasn't afraid to ruin it.

Masaki's kimono was a surprise gift from her parents. She wasn't expecting it, having been saving money on the side. She was reluctant to accept it at first, but her parents smiled and told her, "You're an adult, but you're still our child. You should look nice for today." Masaki laughed thinking back about it. The kimono was beautiful, and she felt breathtaking with it on.

"If you take any longer, we're going to miss the ceremony," moaned Eri.

"Look who's talking," said Masaki. "You don't even care about the ceremony." Masaki rolled her eyes in the mirror making sure Eri saw it.

Eri stuck her tongue out as a reply.

Masaki continued to dress up her face. She wasn't going to let Eri's impatience deter her.

"It's just so boring," cried Eri. "I don't need to sit there for three hours with a bunch of old people telling me that I'm an adult now and I need to step up and be responsible." Eri's voice grew deeper as she spoke, mimicking a professional male.

"I get enough of that from my parents, thank you very

much," she continued. "I've been an adult since I was ten."

"Do you remember when your parents got you that thesaurus for your birthday?" Masaki chuckled.

Eri stared up at the ceiling. She smiled. "…I still have it. It's actually a pretty good thesaurus…"

"How'd that thank you note go?" Masaki asked.

"It was very fastidious," said Eri.

Masaki got up from her chair. She straightened out her kimono and gave herself one last look over in the mirror.

"You look amazing," said Eri.

"It's not too much?" Masaki asked, twirling in the mirror to get a look at her backside. The fabric that draped over her arms waved through the air.

"No," said Eri. "It's perfect."

Masaki shook her head. She was convinced. She was beautiful.

"I bet Koichi will notice," said Eri, raising her eyebrows in a sign of intrigue.

Masaki's face flushed red.

"I bet once he sees you he's going to swoop you up, kiss you on the neck-"

"Shut up," said Masaki. "It's… it's not like that."

"I've seen you looking at him," said Eri. "I can put in a good word."

"Don't you dare say anything!" Masaki's face went from embarrassment to panic in an instant.

Eri laughed, feeling the rush of power of having a secret over

Masaki's head. "Oh, come on, just tell him. He'd be stupid not to say yes."

"We're just friends," said Masaki.

"Not once he sees you in that kimono," said Eri.

Masaki looked back at herself in the mirror. Her face danced with emotions as she admired the kimono.

Masaki shook her head. "We're just friends," she reiterated.

"Get a few drinks in you at the party, we'll see," said Eri with a hint of taunting.

"I don't know about the party," said Masaki.

"No!" Eri said, scrambling off the bed. "No, you said you would go to the party."

"It's just, my parents don't want me going," argued Masaki.

"Then don't tell them," said Eri.

"I haven't," said Masaki. "I haven't. They just know about the party. What if they show up?"

"Why would your parents show up?" Eri questioned. "When have they ever gone to a party? It's three floors down. They aren't going anywhere near it!"

"I just don't like lying to them," said Masaki. "I've done that enough this past year."

"You're an adult," said Eri. "Japan literally says you are an adult now. You are going to the party."

Masaki groaned. Eri came up to her. She wrapped her arms around Masaki's neck as if the two were ready to dance.

"You are going to the party. You are going to have fun! All of our friends are going to be there. Koichi is going to be there."

Masaki involuntarily smiled at the sound of his name. Eri's eyes lit up.

"You're going to the party!" she screamed excitedly.

"I'm going to the party," said Masaki, giving in to her friend's demands.

"You know we can skip the thing entirely," suggested Eri. "Get to the party early."

"No," said Masaki. "I'm going to the party. But we're expected at the ceremony. Our families will be there. I can't skip. You can't skip."

Now, it was Eri's turn to frown. "Fine. But party second!"

"Party second," said Masaki.

Eri closed the gap between the two girls for a strong hug.

"We're adults today!" Eri laughed.

Chapter 4

Masaki and Eri hustled through the busy streets of Tokyo. The Rising Peaks apartment complex was down the street from the nearest train station. It was never a difficult trek, until you were wearing very elegant kimonos.

Masaki took small quick steps. Her dress was snug against the legs, not allowing for much movement. Eri was a different matter. She pushed through the crowd on the streets like a bull. Her kimono brushed and wrinkled against the oncoming tide of the crowd. With one hand she split the crowd of people into two, creating a path, and with the other she dragged Masaki forward by the hand.

"There's Yumiko!" Masaki yelled, trying to direct her friend's charge through the crowd just a bit to the left.

Fujiwara Yumiko sat on the bench of the train station. She sat timidly on one edge of the seat. The other edge was occupied by a man in a suit with his head buried in a newspaper. She kept her head down, not wanting to draw attention to herself. Her dark hair covered much of her face. Only her glasses peeked out allowing Yumiko to see her friend rush into her view.

"You're late," said Yumiko. She scooted just a little bit more to the edge of the bench as if finally talking would draw the attention of the gentlemen next to her.

"You can't rush beauty!" said Eri, sitting down next to Yumiko in the center of the bench. She purposefully sat too close to the man in the suit, leaning up against him. The man grumbled but didn't say a word and walked away. Eri was happy to take the full other half of the bench with her leg.

"I'm sorry, Yumiko," said Masaki. "Have you been here long?"

"No," Yumiko lied. She had been waiting for over twenty minutes, though she didn't blame Masaki. She always liked to be places early. Even if that meant she had to wait a bit.

"Where's Koichi?" Masaki wondered a little too loudly. "And Hisao?" She added to hide her true desire.

Eri gave Masaki a devilish smile. "Not feeling so bad about being late now, huh?"

"I wanted to take a picture before we got on the train," said Yumiko. She held her Polaroid camera in her hand.

"We've still got a few minutes," said Masaki.

The train had not yet arrived. The train station was relatively calm, but in a few short moments there would be no way to sneak in a group photo.

"I love your dress by the way," Masaki said to Yumiko. It was blue with a gold pattern to compliment it.

Yumiko smiled and instinctively hid behind her hair. "Thanks."

"Did you find it at the flea market?" Eri asked.

Yumiko curled up and scooted just a little bit more onto the edge of the bench away from Eri. "No."

"It's looks great," Masaki said again. "You look great." Then she glared at Eri.

Eri shrugged. "I was just kidding. You look good."

Their conversation was interrupted by the sound of the arriving train. Masaki looked around. There was still no sign of Koichi.

"They said they would meet us here," she said out loud.

Eri looked at her watch. "Maybe they are on Koichi time."

Masaki sighed. The one bad thing about Koichi, he was always late.

"Do you think we'll be able to sit together at the ceremony?" Yumiko asked.

"Yeah," said Masaki. "If the guys don't get here in time we'll just have to go ahead and we'll save their seats."

Yumiko smiled. It was reassuring to hear the plan was still in place.

"You mean you could have just saved my seat this whole time?" said Eri. "I could have slept in another two hours."

"It's going to be hard to save seats," said Yumiko. "It's going to be packed."

"We'll do it," said Masaki. "Don't worry."

"What if we don't?" said Yumiko, getting into her own head. "What if we have to be separated?"

"Then we're split up?" said Eri.

"But we should be together," said Yumiko.

"We'll be together," reassured Masaki. She knelt down and took hold of Yumiko's hands. "We're not going anywhere."

Again, Yumiko was able to smile.

Then Eri screamed.

"Aaaaaaahh!"

Her body jolted upward as an arm wrapped around her neck.

Then her screamed turned into laughter.

Mino Hisao held Eri from behind. He wrapped his arms around her waist and nuzzled her neck.

"Hi, everybody!" he beamed.

"You're late," said Eri, finally breaking free from his loving grip. She turned around and planted a kiss on Hisao.

"I should be late more often," said Hisao.

"Don't try it," said Eri. "Where's Koichi?"

Hisao feigned looking at his watch. "He's already there. He got called in last minute to help the staff. Didn't say why."

"Then let's get this party moving!" Eri said, pulling Hisao toward one of the entryways for the train.

The doors opened. A flood of riders rushed out of the train. Eri stood firm, holding onto Hisao, who in turn had Masaki linked in his other arm, followed by Yumiko holding onto Masaki. When the path was clear Eri marched forward, nearly pulling the other three inside the train with her own strength and determination.

"In!" Eri yelled. "On time!" She boasted the last bit toward Yumiko. "Looking good!"

More passengers pushed their way inside the train. Second

by second, the train began to fill up, soon being standing room only. Eri was generous enough to give Masaki and Yumiko the two free seats they had found. She stood next to Hisao, her on and off again boyfriend, with one hand on the train bar the other around Hisao's waist.

"WAIT!"

The voice could be heard across the train station. It went mostly ignored.

Mostly.

"Here comes, Kayo," said Eri, rolling her eyes. "I thought we told him a different time."

"You did," said Masaki. "I told him the right time."

"But why?"

"I didn't want to be mean," said Masaki.

"And that's why Kayo keeps hanging out with us," said Eri.

Okane Kayo rushed through the train station. His tie hung loosely around his neck. His sleeves were rolled up, giving free clearing for the rice bowl in his hands. He shoved his way through the crowd to the train, getting slammed and toppled every few feet.

"Guys!" he shouted as he got closer to the train. "Hold the door! Eri hold the door!"

Eri sluggishly reached out for the door she could not reach without stepping forward. "Oh no," she moaned sarcastically.

But Masaki was there to help. She put her hand on the door, preventing it from closing.

With a boost of confidence, Kayo dashed the last few yards

to get inside the train.

But his speed was too much.

He raised his arms to save his food, sacrificing all his agility.

"Noooooo!" Eri screamed.

His body slammed into the packed house of the train. He teetered on one foot before collapsing. His weight sunk down and he slowly descended onto the floor of the train at the feet of the other passengers.

Hisao broke out in laughter.

Kayo struggled, not being able to get to his feet. Then he noticed his hands were empty. His rice bowl was gone.

Masaki and Yumiko stared off in horror. They didn't dare laugh.

Just a few feet from them, Eri stood motionless. Her glare burned into the soul of Kayo.

Her hair, face, and the front of her kimono were covered by the rice that was once in the hands of the young man.

"I'm… going… to kill you," said Eri.

Kayo tried to smile, but the best he could form was an awkward grin. "I'm sorry."

Eri looked over at Masaki. She would put all the blame on her.

Chapter 5

The air was still crisp in the late morning. Detective Ishida Katashi walked through the light layer of snow on the ground without a second thought. His shoes were comfortable enough, he didn't feel a bit of the cold.

The Gracefields Cemetery was an unusually eerie sight. Katashi was surrounded by the dead, but the cemetery's newest addition was concerning.

The body of the groundskeeper, Yukio, hung from the top of the gated entrance. The man's head was impaled on the spike at the top of the fence's metal framing. Another wound tore away at Yukio's groin. Blood had puddled below him during the night. The snow was dark red.

Katashi looked the body over. It was clear this wasn't suicide. Somebody had done this to the groundskeeper, and he was determined to figure out whom.

The detective readjusted the collar on his jacket, lowering it to let the cold rush over him. He needed a moment to collect his thoughts. He needed to focus. In all of his years as an officer and later a detective he had never seen anything like this. Criminals, kaiju, and everything else in between, but this was something else. This was a monster.

Katashi stepped closer. He took a more detailed look of the wound near the man's crotch. Forensics had already done a quick sweep of the body. They could not immediately identify what the weapon was. Katashi had no better luck.

"Do we know how long he's been here?" Katashi asked.

One of the lab techs, tinkering with some equipment, looked up to address him. "The cold preserved him a bit, but it looks like some time last night."

"Cause of death?" Katashi asked, more out of formality than anything else. The answer was fairly obvious.

"The lower wound," said the forensic lab tech. "He was already dead by the time his head was put on the spike."

Katashi grimaced. He took in another cold breath. They needed to end this quickly.

"Who do you think could do this?" the lab tech asked.

Katashi shook his head. "Somebody very evil."

"Detective! We found something!"

The sound of an officer yelling for Katashi's attention broke his train of thought. The detective turned to the source of the sound. Over a dozen officers were scanning the cemetery for more clues. The snow had left a trail where Yukio's dead body had been dragged. Into the trees and another section of the cemetery was where Katashi was being summoned.

Katashi followed the death trail through the snow. Blood stained the ground at his feet. He was careful to take a second glance at where he was placing his footsteps.

"Give me something good," Katashi said as he approached

the officer.

"We think we found the actual kill sight," said the officer, "but that's not all." He led Katashi through a small gate into another section of the cemetery. Katashi had to brush away the overrun branches that were scraping against his coat.

Once out in the open, Katashi's eyes focused on one point in particular. A black spot poisoned the snowy white landscape of the cemetery. Dirt was overturned. A headstone lay flat on the ground.

"They dug up a body," said the officer.

Crime scene tape surrounded the hole where a coffin was once laid to rest. Splinters of wood were scattered in the snow. Katashi took it all in. He looked at the scene over and over again. There was something nagging at him. Something in the back of his mind, but he couldn't place it. Something wasn't right. He had been there before.

"Have you identified the grave?" Katashi asked.

"Not officially," said the officer. "We're still going through the manifest. This part of the cemetery is for people that were abandoned. No families, some have no names. Very little contact information overall. They were just left to rest here."

Katashi crossed the tape and approached the gravesite. He knelt down to get a closer look at the cracked gravestone. It was small, the name chiseled in the stone was barely legible. He brushed away a bit of the snow and dirt that had accumulated over the night.

Then Katashi's thoughts froze.

He stared at the name, a distant memory broke through the surface.

"Does the manifest have the year when the bodies were put in?" Katashi asked.

"Yeah," said the officer.

Katashi nodded. He looked back down at the gravestone. His fingers traced along the etched in name.

"Find this grave," said Katashi. His voice held an heir of urgency. "Get me everything you can about it."

"Will do," said the officer.

A pain struck Katashi's heart. The pain of failure.

Suddenly, a weight Katashi wasn't expecting to bear again returned. He had failed once fifteen years ago, and a day didn't go by that Katashi didn't see the face of the old man's smile. And the little girl's hands reaching out for help.

Katashi had failed that day. He vowed it would never happen again.

And this case was only a reminder.

He had to find the killer.

The gravestone at the tips of his fingers read: Stan.

Chapter 6

A crowd was formed outside the International House at the Tokyo Metropolitan University. Students and families were slowly piling into the building, ready to welcome the honorees into adulthood.

Yumiko was several steps ahead of Masaki and the others. Having made the train on time, the group of friends was able to breathe easier and travel at a slower leisure. But Yumiko still wanted to make sure they were there on time and had seats together.

Masaki kept close to Eri. Most of Eri's dress was cleaned up, but a notable stain from Kayo's former snack was still visible. Hisao played defense for Kayo. Kayo wanted to clean up the mess, but everyone thought it best to keep the two separated.

"Let me turn around," Eri begged Masaki.

"No," said Masaki. "We're almost there. Nobody is going to notice anyway. You look great."

"I don't believe you," said Eri.

"You look great," Masaki reassured.

Near the entrance, a pair of mittens was waving back and forth. Masaki looked lower to see the beaming face of Sakuma Koichi beckoning his friends to hurry.

Masaki picked up her pace. Eri was pulled forward by her friend's grip. Even Yumiko found herself having to keep up.

"Koichi!" Masaki said on her approach. "Why are you here so early? What's going on?"

"Mr. Haru called me in to help with the preparations," said Koichi. "What happened to your dress?" He pointed at Eri's kimono.

Eri frowned. Her eyes glared at Masaki.

"What did they need your help for?" Masaki said, turning the attention away from Eri's disaster.

"They had a last minute addition and they needed my a/v skills."

"What is it?" Masaki asked.

"Robotman has a special message for all of us!" Koichi announced.

"Robotman!" Kayo gleed. The others were just as excited to hear the mecha-protector of Asia would be addressing their ceremony. He was a hero that most of the city looked up to.

"Punch! Punch! Punch!" Kayo shouted, throwing his fist into the air with every word of the mech's famous catchphrase.

"I will punch your lights out if you keep talking," Eri scolded Kayo.

Kayo dropped his fist. He scuttled slightly behind Hisao for better protection.

"I saved us some seats," said Koichi.

Yumiko's eyes lit up. "Thank you!"

"No problem," said Koichi, "but we should be getting inside.

I don't know how much longer I can hold them. It was as a favor for helping with the video, but that'll wear thin as the crowd comes in."

Yumiko didn't need to be told twice. She started walking without even bothering to be led by Koichi to the seats.

The saved row of seats was near the front. People continued to pile into the auditorium. There was still an hour before the ceremony began. A giant video screen was installed behind the stage. When the video played, Robotman would be almost as large as he was in real life, towering over everybody in attendance.

Yumiko took the first seat in the row. Masaki sat between Koichi and Eri. Then it was Hisao and Kayo at the far end. They were all satisfied and got comfy in conversation.

"Are you going to the party later?" Koichi asked Masaki.

"I think so," answered Masaki. "Eri wants me to go."

"You should," said Koichi. "It'll be fun. The whole apartment is mine for the month."

Voices started to rise as more people filled the auditorium. It would be standing room only in a few short minutes and there was still a lot of time before the ceremony started.

Eri continued to wipe at her dress in the hopes the stain would magically disappear. She huffed when the results were not what she wanted.

"It's okay," said Hisao, in an attempt to calm down his at-the-moment girlfriend.

"No, it's not," said Eri. "I want to get out of here."

"And go where?" Hisao asked.

"Let's just go to the party," said Eri. "We're adults. Yay. I get it. I don't need to be at a ceremony where some old man tells me how responsible I have to take life now."

Hisao shrugged. "I'm down if you are. I don't care about this. I'd love to get to the party early. Get a little pre-game in. Get you out of that kimono."

Eri's ears perked up. Hisao was saying all the right things.

Eri turned to Masaki. "Let's go to the party."

"What? No," said Masaki. "We have to get through the ceremony."

"No, we don't," said Eri. "Let's bail."

"We're not bailing," said Masaki.

Hisao leaned forward and looked across the row at Koichi. "Come on, man. Let's go. Have you seen the Robotman video?"

"Yeah..." Koichi said hesitantly.

"Is it good?"

"It's alright," said Koichi.

"Then we're not missing anything," said Hisao. "Let's go."

Masaki looked back and forth from Koichi to Hisao in disbelief that they were even having the conversation.

"We're not leaving," said Masaki.

"Yeah," said Yumiko. "We have to stay."

"They aren't going to miss us," said Eri. "I'm going."

"Me too," said Hisao. Then he looked over at his friend. "Come on, Koichi. You in?"

Koichi thought about it for a moment. "Yeah, I guess. This is probably going to be boring anyways."

"Yes!" said Hisao.

"I'm in, too!" said Kayo.

Eri's eyes widened. She looked over at Masaki. Her lips mouthed the word 'please.'

"You guys can't go!" said Yumiko. "We were supposed to do this together. What about the picture?"

"Yeah, we need a group picture," said Masaki, trying desperately to get her friends to stay.

Eri rolled her eyes. "Give me your camera." Her hand stuck out with her fingers impatiently waiting for Yumiko's camera.

Yumiko passed the camera over. Then Eri threw it into Kayo's hand.

"Take our picture," she ordered.

Kayo fumbled with the camera. He tried to reach out his

arm and point the camera at all of them sitting together in the row. But the others complained.

"You're going to mess it up!" Eri said.

"You're doing it all wrong!" said Hisao.

"This is for Yumiko," said Koichi.

Then Kayo readjusted. He got out of his seat and stood awkwardly between the two rows. He was no longer in the picture, but the others could now pose with confidence that the group photo would be nice.

"Say, Punch! Punch! Punch!" said Kayo.

"Cheese!" everybody said instead.

A flash hit their eyes. The picture was taken.

Eri grabbed the camera from Kayo's hands and handed it back to Yumiko.

"Picture taken," said Eri. "Can we go now?"

Masaki looked back over at Yumiko. Then she looked at Koichi.

Eri, Hisao, and Kayo were out of their chairs.

Koichi began to stand up.

"I'm sorry, Yumiko," said Masaki. "I'm going to go with them. You should come to."

Yumiko kept her head down. "No, that's okay. I'm going to stay."

"Do you want me to stay with you?" Masaki asked.

"No, you're fine," said Yumiko with a low voice. "I'll join you guys later."

"Are you sure?" said Masaki, now on her feet.

"Yeah," said Yumiko. "Have fun."

Masaki smiled. "I'll see you later at the party."

"Yeah," said Yumiko.

"Awesome," said Koichi. "Let's go."

Eri waited for Masaki and Koichi at the end of the row. Her arms were wide open to accept a congratulatory hug for Masaki's misdeed.

"This is being an adult," said Eri. "Doing what you want. Let's go have some fun!"

Then the five friends hurried out of the auditorium, away from the rushed crowd, and back to their home where the party awaited.

Chapter 7

Ishida Katashi drove aimlessly for nearly an hour. At first, it was just a long drive due to the traffic. Then he slipped into the rabbit hole of his thoughts. His turn came and went.

The news he had received moments before beginning his drive was settling in. His thoughts went back to fifteen years ago. He could never forget walking through the retirement home while the building crumbled around him.

But all that was nothing compared to what he saw in that room. The blood had stained every wall, all the way up to the ceiling. And the man's smile. The satisfied look of a job well done mixed with his dead eyes. Katashi had never seen anything like it.

Stan was evil.

There was no other explanation.

After Matamerra's destruction, Katashi spent time looking up the history of Stan. To his dismay, there wasn't much.

Stan didn't have a history. His family checked him in one day and they never returned. He was a ghost among the living.

Katashi reached out to the family, hoping they could shed some light on Stan, but they never responded to any of Katashi's calls.

There was only one person that ever bothered to answer Katashi's questions about Stan, and it just happened to be Kawahara Kyo, the head nurse at the retirement home before it was destroyed. She was more than happy to gossip about her least favorite resident. And Katashi was not afraid to use the last few moments inside the retirement home as leverage. The death of Emi was a burden they both shared in secret.

Kawahara Kyo was the head administrating nurse at the retirement home. She had worked there for over thirty years. It was joked she had actually retired and was just living there still giving the orders. Her tongue could keep everybody in line, either with a generous compliment or a harsh lashing. She kept the gossip flowing, learning everything she could about the residents. And she wasn't afraid to trash on those she needed to.

When she first spoke with Katashi after the incident, she was not at a loss for words. "Always gave me the creeps," she began. "I felt bad for him at first. You always see it eventually. The family comes every day. Then once a week. Then every couple of weeks. Eventually months go by and they don't stop by. Then one day is their last visit. They say they can't wait to come back and see them. They don't. That's usually when we start keeping an extra eye on them. They'll be gone within six months. Nothing left to live for.

"But Stan, sheesh, his daughter dropped him off, we never saw her again. The paperwork was minimal. She didn't go into detail about her father, his interest, or anything like that."

"I stopped feeling bad about the whole thing once I got to

know Stan. Or got to know his habits. He barely spoke. He mostly grumbled. Mumbled curse words under his breath. He bit several of the nurses. He tolerated me for some reason. Meaning I had to deal with him the most.

"The man was just pent up hatred for the world. His medication made him docile. I was more than happy to force feed him that. It stopped the biting and any further abuse to the staff.

"The world will not miss Stan. That's all you need to know. You saw what he did to that family. He killed them all."

"Not all of them…" Katashi's voice trailed off.

"Stan killed all of them," Kyo said matter-of-factly. "Do not shed a tear for that murderer. His family had already let him go. He deserved what happened to him."

Katashi let it end there. His curiosity of Stan would have to be satisfied with that answer. And over the years, Katashi's thoughts on Stan faded. He became just a nuisance in the back of his thoughts. But he never forgot about the girl.

Until today.

The name on the cemetery stone brought back all those old memories.

And fate found a way to pique Katashi's curiosity once again.

The vandalized gravesite that was found early that morning did in fact belong to the same Stan.

Katashi had gone to the funeral. There was no open casket ceremony. Even if Stan's body had not been obliterated by Matamerra nobody would have shown up anyway to pay respects.

Why would anybody desecrate his grave? Take his remains?

Those questions circled around Katashi's mind so much he hadn't realized where he had gone. He was driving through a quaint neighborhood in the outskirts of Tokyo. The neighborhood was a complete contrast of the busy life in the city. It was perfect for somebody to retire and spend the rest of their lives.

That was exactly what Kawahara Kyo did.

Katashi pulled up to the old woman's home. He just wanted to drive by, rehearse what he was going to say while he found a parking spot. He didn't know what Kyo would be able to offer him now. Stan had been dead for fifteen years. Kyo wouldn't know why anybody would dig up the man's body.

As Katashi passed the former nurse's home he noticed the front door of the house was ajar. Unusual to say the least.

A nearby spot was clear for Katashi to park. He walked to the house with a brisk pace. He hoped to catch Kyo while she was still at the door. He was sure Kyo would laugh when he told her the news. She'd say Stan deserved what happened.

Katashi approached the entrance of the house. There was nobody at the door.

"Kyo!" Katashi called out. "Hello!" He knocked on the door.

There was no answer.

The house was quiet. Katashi took a step inside. His footsteps creaked against the hardwood floor.

"Kyo," Katashi said again. "This is Detective Katashi. It's been a while. Do you remember me? After the retirement home was destroyed. I spoke with you about the murders. Stan?"

Still no reply from the deathly silent home.

She was absent from the living room.

Katashi made a path to the kitchen. Kyo was not there.

The backdoor was in clear view and Katashi's heart raced. The door was splintered. It had been forced open. There was a fresh dent in the wall behind it.

Katashi went to full alert. He called out once again for the retired nurse. There was no sign of a burglary. No vandalism.

He rushed to the hallway. Several doors were laid out. Katashi checked each one as he passed them. The bathroom was clear. The guest bedroom was empty.

The last door was down at the end of the hall.

"Kyo! It's Detective Katashi. Are you there?"

Katashi came up to the room. The door was half way open. He nudged it back, entering the master bedroom.

He let out a small sigh of relief. Kyo was sitting on an arm chair looking out the window.

But Katashi was not satisfied yet. There were two doors in the house that were broken and left open. Something wasn't right.

He quickly approached the chair. The room was empty except for them two.

Katashi came into full view of Kyo.

Then he took a step back.

Kyo was dead. Two small wounds sunk into her head where her eyes used to be. Kyo's mouth hung open, her tongue ripped out. A large wound was in the center of her chest. Blood stained her dress and the chair she was sitting in.

Tears of blood reached down her face. She was positioned to be looking out the window at the view of the neighborhood. Outside, a family was playing in their front yard, unaware a dead woman was keeping an eye on them.

Katashi's heart began to race. The wound was similar to the groundskeeper at the cemetery.

It couldn't be a coincidence.

Kyo's dead gaze remained at the window.

Katashi was taken back to Stan's dead eyes smiling back at him.

There was no explanation for what was going on.

But something evil was emerging, and Katashi had to find a way to stop it.

Chapter 8

Masaki stood sheepishly in a corner phone booth, crammed inside with Eri. Eri forced the phone into Masaki's hands. Their friends were waiting outside, some more impatient than others.

"Make the call!" said Hisao.

"Chill!" Eri yelled back at her boyfriend. "She will."

Eri turned her attention back to Masaki. "It's just a phone call."

"I can't keep lying to my parents like this," said Masaki.

"It's fine," said Eri. "They won't find out."

"What if it's too late?" Masaki asked. "What if they are already at the ceremony looking for me?"

"They aren't," said Eri. "I know your parents. They do not leave for things until the proper time."

Masaki's stomach dropped. She knew Eri was right. Her parents were sticklers for schedules. Even leaving early could throw off the entire day.

"I'll dial," said Eri. She punched in the numbers for Masaki's apartment. Masaki froze. She wanted to stop Eri, but her body wouldn't move.

Then the ringing chimed in her ear.

Eri lit up. It was the moment of truth.

"Hello?" said Masaki's mother over the telephone line.

Masaki's voice disappeared. Her mouth was wide open but she couldn't utter a word.

Eri forced down her laughter. She urged Masaki to say something.

"Hello?" Masaki's mother said again. "Is somebody there?"

Eri fake coughed. The noise was loud enough to be heard over the phone.

Masaki panicked.

"Who is this?"

"Mom, hi!" said Masaki, with rapid speed.

"Masaki? What was that?"

"Nothing," said Masaki.

Eri glared at Masaki.

"No," said Masaki. "It... some people are sick."

"Sick?"

"Yeah, they are cancelling the ceremony," lied Masaki. "One of the speakers is sick, they don't want to spread it to anybody else. They are worried it's that kaiju-virus, Thill."

"Oh, no!"

"Yeah," said Masaki. "They want to be careful. So, the ceremony is cancelled. You don't have to come down here."

"Are you okay?" spoke up another voice, Masaki's dad. "Have you gotten sick? Are you washing your hands? That's how those viruses get you."

"Yes, dad," said Masaki. "I am careful."

"Good," said her dad. "It's bad enough that a bunch of people are piling into the building today. I can hear them in the hallways."

"It's just some parties," said Masaki.

"They should party at their own place, not here," said her dad. "They have homes too."

"Yeah, dad," said Masaki, not willing to argue with her parents.

"I want you to come home if the ceremony is cancelled," said her mother. "You should lie down in case you are sick. I'll make some noodles."

"Come home?" Masaki said with panic. Wide eyes stared back at Eri. Eri shook her head. Her ruse worked too well.

"I'll be home as-," began Masaki.

Then Eri panicked. She grabbed the phone from Masaki's hands and slammed it down on the cradle.

Masaki and Eri stared at each other in silence. Worried the phone would ring, somehow controlled by her parent's concerns.

"It worked?" Eri asked. "They're not going?"

"You hung up on them," said Masaki.

"You can say the phone line got cut," said Eri.

"You hung up on them," said Masaki again. "I am in so much trouble."

"Then have some fun before that," said Eri. She slid the door to the phone booth open. With ease she pulled Masaki out with her.

"We are ready to go!" Eri announced.

Hisao stepped up and gave Masaki a big hug. "I knew you could do it!"

"That's my girl," said Eri.

Masaki still did not respond. She had never defied her parents before. She could not comprehend it yet.

Then Koichi came up and put his arm around Masaki's shoulders. He gave her a hug and a reassuring hold.

"It's not that bad," said Koichi. "If your parents get mad, just tell them I needed your help with the equipment tear down. That'll soften the blow."

Masaki nodded her head. Koichi's words were less important than his confidence. She felt safe with him.

"Let's have some fun," said Koichi.

Masaki smiled. She was going to make the most of her first day as an adult.

Across the city, the familiar tone of a cut off phone line blared in Masaki's parent's ears. Yoshiaki and Shinju, tried to call out for their daughter, in the hopes the phone would reconnect.

It did not.

"I'm sure she'll be home soon," said Masaki's mother, Shinju.

"She better not be bringing any kind of cold into the apartment," said Yoshiaki. "She's going straight to her room when she gets here. Get some soup going."

Shinju nodded and headed for the kitchen.

Then another loud noise echoed through the hallway.

Yoshiaki stirred. He hated the muffled sounds of people talking. It was just audible enough to hear a few words, but not enough to hear the entire conversation. It drove him crazy. He would have even preferred cheaper walls that allowed the whole conversation to come through. Louder, sure, but at least he would be able to process what was being said.

The only other alternative was to tell people to keep it down out in the hallway. Loud chatter and screams were uncalled for in any social setting.

"Oh, leave them be," said Shinju when she saw her husband heading for the door.

"I live here," said Yoshiaki. "They don't. I have a right to peace and quiet."

Shinju rolled her eyes. She wasn't going to stop her husband with any argument.

Yoshiaki opened the door. The hallway was empty.

Yoshiaki grumbled. Then he shut the door.

"Who was it?" Shinju asked.

"Nobody," said Yoshiaki. "They're gone now."

Then music began to blare, vibrating the walls to the beat of the melody.

Yoshiaki dropped his shoulders. The noise could be coming from anywhere.

He rushed over to the door again. With anger fueled force he swung it open. He was going to find the perpetrator of the music. He wasn't going to stand for it.

But something was in his way.

The hallway was blocked by the imposing figure of a grotesque being, almost seven feet tall. Skin pale as death, with red veins that could be seen through the surface. Its head came down to drooping tentacles over its mouth. And its hands were twisted and cuffed around a sickle of bones. Sharp spikes swung from the monster's arms like pendulums.

Yoshiaki screamed, but his voice was drowned out by the music blaring from another apartment.

Stan charged forward into the home. Its arms swung out piercing Yoshiaki in the stomach. Blood splattered onto a family picture welcoming guests into the apartment.

The door closed behind the horrific creature.

Their final screams would not be heard.

Chapter 9

Katashi took a sip of his coffee while he waited in the back of the crime scene lab. Since returning from Kawahara Kyo's home, Katashi was on the hunt for answers. He didn't want to waste a second, but all he could do was wait for lab results to come in.

Katashi grumbled, loud enough for the technician to hear it. He took another sip of his coffee, only slightly aware that his cup was empty. The few drops that made it into his mouth did not satisfy his unquenchable drive.

"Anything?" Katashi spoke up.

The lab technician, Jun, rolled his eyes. "Not since you asked twenty minutes ago."

"Jun, I need something," said Katashi. "Two people are dead. A body goes missing, and the one person even vaguely connected to it is murdered. This is something."

"Vaguely connected," said Jun. "You're grasping at straws. Maybe it's time to retire."

"I don't need to retire," said Katashi. "I need answers. Something strange is going on. I can feel it."

"It was a grave robbery gone wrong," said Jun. "That's it.

Strange? Yes. But nothing nefarious. Just some vandalization that somebody needed to cover up."

"Cover up with murder," reminded Katashi.

"Right," said Jun. "But that doesn't mean it's a serial killer or something. Here, come look at this."

Katashi groaned as he walked toward Jun.

"This was a lot messier than we originally thought," began Jun. "The casket was ripped apart. See these lines here."

Jun pointed out ridges along the debris of the casket. Katashi did not know what he was looking at.

"They are from the inside of the casket. Whoever did this must have ripped open the door and then started to destroy it. This wasn't about the body or the murder. They were just looking to destroy things. The groundskeeper shows up at the wrong place and the wrong time."

"Broken from the inside?" Katashi double checked.

"Yeah," said Jun. "Like it was ripped apart."

Katashi froze, lost in thought.

"What?" Jun asked.

"What if it was busted from the inside?" Katashi wondered out loud.

"What?" Jun laughed. "Like this Stan guy got up and broke himself out of his grave?"

Katashi kept staring at the broken piece of wood. The ridge smiled back at him. The same eerie smile that was on Stan's face the last time Katashi had seen him.

"Maybe," said Katashi.

"That's out of my jurisdiction," said Jun. "Same for you. It's vandalism. It's murder. Nothing more."

"I hope you're right," said Katashi, not settled with the answers Jun was giving him.

Chapter 10

Masaki's arm was wrapped around Eri's as they returned to the apartment complex. Masaki's eyes darted back and forth, watching out for any sign of her parents. One wrong hallway and the party would be over.

Hisao jumped ahead of the group and opened the front door for his friends. He bowed as he held the door open as if he was the doorman for an upscale hotel.

Masaki did a quick double take.

"Did somebody leave the door unlocked?" she asked Hisao.

"It was just propped open, I don't know," he answered. He let go of the handle, allowing the door to swing back into place.

A soft clink echoed in the entry way of the apartment building.

The group of friends kept walking, Masaki looked back. She couldn't be sure, but it looked like the door to the main entrance was bent, forcing it to stay unlocked.

But her worries were pushed aside as Eri and the others pulled Masaki into the elevator that would take them to a night they would never forget.

The fourteenth floor was buzzing with activity. Several parties had spilled out of their respective apartments and mingled in the hallway. The group made a beeline to their particular party at Koichi's place. Koichi's older brother had already started the festivities. His parents were out of the country for the month. It was the perfect time to celebrate.

As soon as Masaki entered the party she turned to Eri to find her already with a drink in her hand. Eri smiled at her friend then let out a quick "Woooo!" Several girls across the room replied in kind, kicking the party into a higher gear for a moment.

"I told you this would be fun," Eri said to Masaki.

Masaki shook her head, still uneasy about ditching the ceremony.

"Lighten up!" Eri cried. "Get a drink. Talk to Koichi."

"I lied to my parents," said Masaki. "What if they find out? What if they come down here?"

"They won't!" said Eri. "Besides, you're an adult now! You can do whatever you want!"

"I don't feel like an adult," said Masaki. Her voice trailed off to morose thoughts. She felt alone at the party. Nobody could understand the hollow feeling in her stomach that was crying out. Masaki wanted to leave. She wanted to return to the ceremony and apologize to her parents.

But Eri took her hand and walked her through the crowded party. They stopped at the entryway of the balcony. Koichi and Hisao were outside leaning against the balcony's ledge, drinks in their hands.

"I saw you guys chatting earlier," said Eri. "Get in there."

"I… I can't," said Masaki, hesitant to move forward.

Eri groaned. She rolled her eyes to an exaggerated degree. It was the same excuse from Masaki. Every time.

"He likes you," said Eri, cutting off Masaki before she could get in another word.

"What?" Masaki said.

"Koichi likes you. Hisao told me so," said Eri. "I wasn't supposed to tell anybody. Hisao wasn't supposed to tell anybody, either. But, what can you do?"

"Koichi likes me," Masaki repeated with uncertainty.

"Yes," said Eri. "So go over there and tell him you like him too. We're all just waiting for you two to hook up already. It's nauseating that it hasn't happened yet."

"Oh," said Masaki, thrown off by Eri's words. "I don't know. What if he doesn't like me anymore? What if I took too long?"

Eri rolled her eyes once again. Then she shook her head.

"Nope. Not this time," Eri said. She turned and walked out onto the balcony.

"Hisao!" Eri called out. "There you are!"

She cradled under Hisao's arm. Then she looked over at Masaki and nodded for her to join them.

Koichi smiled when he saw Masaki approach the group.

"Did you get a drink?" he asked Masaki.

"No," she replied.

"I can get you one," said Koichi.

"That's okay," she answered.

"Okay," said Koichi, defeated in his generosity.

"Hisao," said Eri. "This drink isn't great. Can you make me one? You know I love your stuff."

"Sure," said Hisao with a gleaming smile.

Masaki went wide eyed. She glared at Eri who was smiling back at her friend.

"What do you want?" Hisao asked. He started to pull away from Eri, but Eri held on.

"I'll join you," said Eri. "We can make something together."

Her words were followed by a slap of Hisao's butt that got him moving at a faster pace.

"We'll be back!" Hisao shouted.

"Maybe!" Eri added as the two of them returned inside the apartment. They soon vanished into the crowd of party goers.

Masaki looked up at Koichi. They both smiled but stayed silent for a moment.

Finally, Koichi spoke up.

"Are you sure you don't want a drink?" he asked.

"No," said Masaki.

"Hisao makes good ones," said Koichi.

"I'm good," said Masaki.

Koichi responded with a head nod.

The silence returned.

Masaki's attention diverted back to the party. She could see Eri and Hisao by the bar. She laughed at something Hisao was saying. Masaki couldn't help but feel jealous.

Then Kayo poked his head up out of the crowd near Eri and

Hisao. Quickly, all attention went to the self titled prankster.

"What's he doing?" Koichi asked as he too was drawn into Kayo's latest call for attention.

Kayo stood on top of a chair. One foot balancing on the top of the back while the other was on the seat. He tilted forward bringing two of the chair's legs off of the ground.

The crowd cheered at Kayo's amazing feat.

Then just as quickly, Kayo lost his balance. His arms swung wildly in the air in a desperate attempt to regain his composure. The chair dipped to its side, abandoning all hope of staying upright.

Masaki and Koichi watched helplessly from the balcony. It became obvious what was about to happen.

Kayo fell forward toward the bar. Eri had no place to escape. She screamed as Kayo fell in front of her. His flailing arms struck the freshly made drink in her hand.

Bright blue alcohol splashed into the air, spilling all over Eri. Her hair, her face, her dress, all covered in the delicious fruity cocktail Hisao had concocted.

Kayo crashed onto the floor with a loud thud. The crowd laughed and cheered in the delight of his pain. Eri's collateral damage was only the cherry on top for the onlookers.

Kayo stumbled to regain his composure on the ground. He looked up. Eri glared at him. Her hands were at her side. The empty cup turned upside down. There was nothing left to pour out. Alcohol dripped from her face and hair.

Eri growled.

"I'm…" Kayo tried to get out, but it was too late.

Eri threw the empty cup at the fallen Kayo.

"You idiot!" Eri yelled. "Look what you did! My dress is completely ruined. Again! By you!"

She lunged at Kayo, but Hisao was quick to the draw. He wrapped his arms around Eri and held her back. Kayo scurried away several feet. The crowd around him continued to laugh and point in Kayo's direction.

"It's okay, it's okay," said Hisao.

"No, it's not okay!" yelled Eri. "What is he even doing here? Nobody actually invited him. He just shows up. He shouldn't be here!"

Kayo frowned. Eri's words hurt him harder than the fall from the chair. He couldn't look her in the eyes anymore.

Slowly, Kayo got to his feet. He kept his head down. He didn't need to see that Eri continued to glare at him. The laughter from the crowd was infectious. Kayo couldn't get it out of his head.

Kayo stood silent and still.

"Go!" Eri yelled. "Get out of here!"

Kayo swallowed hard. He tried his best to hold off the tears that wanted to pour down his face. He sniffed air through his nose and began his walk toward the exit.

Eri shook her head. Her breaths were deep with fury. Hisao loosened his grip around her. What was once a restraining hold turned into a gentle hug.

"You should change," suggest Hisao. "I can help."

Eri shook her head. She couldn't hold back a smile. Hisao always knew the right thing to say.

She waited for Kayo to leave the apartment. Once Eri felt the coast was clear, she took Hisao by the hand and led him away. Her apartment was just down the hall.

Masaki watched, stunned that Eri was now leaving the party. That left her alone with Koichi. It should have been a dream come true.

"Where are they going?" Koichi wondered.

"Maybe I should go with her?" Masaki wondered.

"No," said Koichi.

Masaki looked up at Koichi. They stared into each other eyes.

"Hisao is with her," said Koichi. "I'm sure they're fine."

"Yeah," said Masaki with a smile.

"Do you want to take a walk?" asked Koichi. "Let the vibe here cool down."

"I'd like that," said Masaki, surprised she got the words out.

Koichi smiled back. He took the first step away from the ledge of the balcony. Masaki followed.

They would soon get some proper time to be alone together.

Chapter 11

Ishida Katashi moaned at the sound of the phone line telling him that his call was still on hold. He had been transferred three times already and the fourth wasn't going any quicker. He had been on hold for forty minutes. The call was being sent to the office of Captain Hashimoto Akane. She was one of the liaisons between the Tokyo police department and K.A.R.R.D. The organization specialized in not only kaiju attacks but any other happenstance that is considered outside the norm for the police department.

Katashi had forced his suspicions through the first few levels of contact, but it wasn't without pulling teeth and this was the latest roadblock. It would seem Captain Hashimoto was out of the office.

Finally, the line picked up.

Katashi froze for a moment, suddenly unprepared in the event he actually got through.

"This is Captain Hashimoto," said the stern woman's voice on the other end. "Who is this?"

"Hello, this is Detective Ishida Katashi with the Tokyo Police Department. I have been trying to get through to somebody all morning. I have a problem that needs back up from K.A.R.R.D."

"If it's a case that needs to be bumped up there are proper channels for that," dismissed Hashimoto.

"No!" said Katashi. "The proper channels don't want to follow up."

"Then they believe you can handle the case," replied Hashimoto.

"This is beyond me," said Katashi. "Something strange is happening. This is supernatural territory."

"If my men have deemed it not a supernatural threat then I would take their opinion on it."

"Your men are wrong," said Katashi.

"I have my absolute faith in my team, Detective Ishida."

"Just hear me out," said Katashi.

"If my team has already passed on the case then I will do the same," warned Hashimoto.

"Damn it, just listen!" said Katashi. "A grave was destroyed the other night. From the inside. The body missing. Yesterday, a woman connected to the person in the grave was found dead. I found her dead. Something is going on!"

"That is not enough to indicate a supernatural occurrence," said Hashimoto. "It sounds like vandalism and the poor timing of a death."

"A body is missing!" said Katashi, stunned that Captain Hashimoto was dismissing him as easily as her subordinates.

"Which is a job for the police department," said Hashimoto.

"Who else can I talk to?" asked Katashi.

"Nobody," said Hashimoto. "This is the end of the line. Stop wasting my department's time. Good day."

The phone line went dead.

Katashi sat at his desk and mulled in the sound of the phone in his ear.

Nobody wanted to listen. Nobody wanted to do anything.

But Katashi wanted to do something. He had to.

Chapter 12

Kayo wandered aimlessly a floor above the party. His tears were mostly dry, but the humiliation of falling over at the party still stung deep. He could still hear the feint sounds of music blasting through the floor below him, and the hushed tones of dozens of conversations trying to talk over the other.

He had practiced his balance on the smooth floor. He nailed his positioning. What had gone wrong on the chair?

Kayo took in several deep breaths. He forced a smile on his face. All he needed was a clever line to return with. Then the party would welcome him back.

He practiced opening a door. Then he rushed forward a few steps along the hallway. "I'm back!"

Then Kayo shook his head. That wasn't the line.

"See you next fall!"

Kayo shook his head. He had to go bigger. So big even Eri couldn't yell at him.

Then it hit him.

Robotman!

"Punch, Punch, Punch!"

Kayo shouted in the hallway, swinging his fist with the rhythm of his words.

Kayo had it! He was going to enter the party larger than life. Once he yelled Robotman's famous catchphrase, the others at the party would chant with him. It was that simple.

Kayo smiled. He was going to be the talk of the party yet.

With a renewed energy, Kayo turned for the stairwell. He threw his fist several more times into the air while reciting Robotman's catch phrase in his head. He even thought about adding a little jump when he punched. It would let everyone in the apartment know he was there.

Kayo turned around and pushed the stairwell door open with his back. This allowed him to send a flurry of imitation punches.

"Punch, Punch,-"

Stab.

Kayo froze.

His stomach ripped with pain. A sudden surge of warm blood drowned his throat.

Kayo looked down. His hands braced up against a boney protrusion emanating from his stomach. Blood caked the sharp object. Kayo's blood.

Weakly, Kayo turned his head. There was no pain to stop him. His body was numb. He could feel blood dribbling down his chin.

Behind Kayo was the grotesque face of Stan. Two red eyes looked down at the young man. Short tentacles dangled from the monster's face, covering its neck. Stan tilted his head as if examining the dying light of Kayo.

Kayo tried to scream, but the blood in his throat prevented any hope of salvation.

Stan raised his right arm. Two red boney scythe-like spikes were at the other end in place of a hand. It hung in the air for just a moment. Long enough for Kayo's eyes to go wide. His fate was laid out before him.

Stan brought down his bladed hand.

The spike cut into Kayo's neck, tore through his chest and came out from the stomach on his right.

The clean cut left Kayo's upper body to slide away from his waist and tumble to the floor. His legs were not far behind.

Stan stared silently at his work. Kayo lay in two piles of flesh and blood.

Then Stan pierced Kayo's body, using his scythe like a fork.

The monster made his way down the stairwell, Kayo's body in tow.

Masaki and Koichi walked aimlessly through the hallways of the apartment complex. It was much quieter on the other side of the building. The sounds of the party were gone. Though Masaki did have to keep an eye out for her parents, every moment she was with Koichi she seemed less concerned about that.

"Will your parents be mad you didn't attend the ceremony?" Koichi asked.

"Probably," said Masaki. "Hopefully they didn't go."

"I'm sorry I made you leave," said Koichi. "I didn't mean to get you into any trouble."

"Don't feel sorry," said Masaki. "I chose to leave. I wanted to join you."

"Yeah?" asked Koichi.

"Yeah," said Masaki. She brushed up against him. For a second their arms felt each other's embrace.

"Do you feel any different? You know, as an adult?" Koichi

asked. "My parents keep telling me, it's time to start a career. Get back into engineering. Leave the video stuff in my past."

"Are you?" Masaki asked.

"I don't want to," said Koichi. "I don't feel like an adult. I don't need to all of a sudden get an office job and leave my dreams behind. That's what my parents want."

"Maybe they know what's best," said Masaki.

"How could they know?" said Koichi. "How do any adults know? We're adults now. I have no idea what I am doing."

"Me either," laughed Masaki.

"When do we figure it out?" Koichi sighed.

"According to my parents, ten years ago," Masaki chuckled. "They're the ones that pushed me into nursing school. They said it would be a good foundation for the rest of my life."

"Do you believe that?" Koichi asked.

"I suppose," said Masaki. "I don't hate it. And it's nice to help people."

Koichi stopped. He turned to look directly at Masaki.

"But it's not what you want?" he asked her, staring into her brown eyes.

"I don't know what I want," said Masaki. A part of her wanted to recoil. Koichi was very close to her. She didn't know what she was going to do.

"What do you want?" Koichi asked.

"I… I want… I just want to be happy," said Masaki. "Sometimes I think it doesn't matter what I do for a job. I just want to spend time with the people I love. My family and friends."

She stepped closer to Koichi as she said her words. Without realizing it, her hands gently grabbed on to his arms.

"My parents hate their jobs. I think they barely like each other," continued Masaki. "I don't want to be like that. I don't want to be miserable."

Then Koichi leaned forward. It was so fast neither he nor Masaki registered what was going on until after their lips parted.

Masaki blushed behind a smile.

Koichi stepped back, embarrassed by his actions.

"I'm sorry," he said. "I didn't mean… I just… I'm sorry."

"No," said Masaki. "It's okay."

She stepped forward to once again be close to Koichi.

"I like you," she said, relief washed over her, her feelings no longer crushing her.

Masaki took hold of Koichi's hands. Then she leaned in for another kiss.

It was gentle and passionate this time; two lovers finally giving in to their desires.

Chapter 13

The area was completely different than the last time Ishida Katashi was there. Rising Peaks Apartments raised high into the air. It wasn't like that all those years ago at the Keiro Gardens. You used to be able to see the city skyline and Mt. Fuji on the horizon. Now, it would seem you had to pay for that.

The door to the front entrance was broken. Katashi stopped to examine it. There was no indication what had broken the door. Several groups of young adults walked freely in and out of the building. They didn't have a care in the world. None of them even stopped to notice the broken door. There was no danger in their eyes. They were untouchable for the moment.

Ishida Katashi grumbled as he pushed his way inside the building. He noticed the unusual flow of foot traffic in the lobby. The room was full with several clusters of people. Katashi was the only one that stood alone.

"What's going on today?" he asked openly to the group closest to him.

"Just a party, old man," said a guy who couldn't have been older than seventeen. He laughed at the insult toward Katashi. He wore a suit half tucked in.

"It's Coming of Age Day!" said a young girl in the group. Her kimono was still nicely put together.

Katashi nodded. He had forgotten. Not that it was an important day to him. He didn't have kids, and he was long past coming of age.

The elevator door opened. Another group of young adults poured out into the lobby. Katashi noted all of the formal wear. And all of the blood shot eyes.

"Thank you," he said to the group that he was talking to as he entered the elevator. "Be careful out there. Understand? If you see anything suspicious, I'll be around."

The group laughed. They didn't take Katashi's warning seriously.

"Whatever!" Then the young guy that had insulted Katashi earlier gave the detective the middle finger.

Katashi rolled his eyes.

Youth was wasted on the young.

He pushed the button for the second floor. Katashi grimaced. He didn't have a plan. It was just a gut feeling that brought him to Rising Peaks. This was where Stan used to live, it stood to reason he would return there.

Katashi just wanted a look around. That wasn't going to be easy in an apartment complex, especially one with hundreds of people milling about. But he could feel it. Something was close by. Something terrible was on the horizon.

After several floors of searching, Katashi stumbled onto the fourteenth floor where the party was at. He walked through a crowd of bumbling young party goers. The music blared, leaving him to concentrate and look for anything suspicious in the area.

It had been years since he'd been to a party like that. A part of him wondered what had happened. He used to drink with the best of them. There would be many nights that ended at dawn. He shrugged it off. Those were just the good old days. He eventually got settled in a career. But the destruction he saw day in and day out wasn't easy. So much death. What was the point in the end? Everything ended in heartache. Finally, he made detective, but the job just got worse from there. He was put face to face with the evils of the world every day. Katashi would often think about quitting, but then he'd see Stan's smile again, and he knew he had to push on. His career would end, and end soon, he was beginning to think, but he would push on for as long as he could. There were still wrongs to right.

Katashi could control one thing in this world and that was his life. He did things on his terms now. He could look back and at least be happy about that.

He ignored the smirks from the party goers. They saw him and thought he was a joke. Others took one look at Katashi and bolted. He wasn't hiding the fact that he was a cop. But he wasn't there to knock anybody down for drugs or anything like that. His mind was focused.

He had to find Stan.

Just down the hall, the music still hummed through the

walls. Eri bobbed her head to the beat. Her vodka stained kimono was on her bed. She paced across her room in just her underwear, much to the delight of Hisao. He sat at Eri's desk. The swivel chair was almost as exciting as her walking around half naked.

Eri still fumed about Kayo. She huffed every time her eyes crossed over her dress.

"What am I supposed to wear now?" she thought out loud. "I have nothing for the party."

Hisao laughed. "You have a whole closet full of clothes. Just pick one."

Eri glared at Hisao. "I can't just pick one. I'm not going to just throw something on like a bum. Look at you. You've got a tie, a jacket. Your shoes are even shined!"

Hisao looked down at his formal wear. He shrugged. The tie was loose around his neck. His shirt wasn't tucked in. One of his shoelaces was even untied.

"And you don't even care!" Eri screamed. "Boys!"

Hisao laughed again. He didn't know what she was getting worked up about.

"I'd be happy to match with you," he said. Then he took off his jacket.

Eri stopped pacing. She stared at Hisao. He was unbuttoning his shirt.

"No," said Eri. "Don't do that."

"Too late," said Hisao. He dropped his shirt to the floor. The next things to go were his shoes. His one loose shoe soared into the air with a simple flick of the foot. His other shoes had to be pried off.

"Stop," said Eri.

"Come on," said Hisao. He visually whimpered into Eri's eyes.

She shook her head, giving in to Hisao's request.

"Fine," she said.

"Can I get some help here?" he asked.

Eri smiled. She rushed up to him on the desk chair. The two of them swiveled back and forth as Eri settled on Hisao's lap.

As she kissed him, her hands reached down for Hisao's belt buckle. Quickly, she had it undone and slid away from his pants.

"You are so hot," he said between breaths.

Eri grinded up against Hisao. She forced her frustration out.

Then a noise broke up the tension. Eri stopped. She looked at the doorway to her room. The disturbance sounded close.

"What was that?" she asked.

Hisao hadn't been listening, but he answered anyway. "It was nothing."

"I heard a weird bump," said Eri.

"It's the party," said Hisao. He kissed Eri along the neck. His hands brushed against every inch of her body.

"Are you sure?" Eri asked.

"It's probably Kayo doing more stupid stuff," said Hisao. "I bet he's got a new gag to make everybody laugh."

Eri rolled her eyes. The intense hatred returned, driving her more to move, to get the energy out of her.

"Freaking Kayo," she mumbled.

"Yeah, screw him," said Hisao. He pulled Eri in tight as they continued to hold close.

Then Eri got back to her feet. Hisao reached out for her. His eyes followed her slender body as she walked over to the bed.

Eri brushed aside the once important kimono. It crumbled to the floor in a heap. Her eyes were on Hisao.

"I thought you were going to dress like me?" she said.

Hisao did not hesitate. He fumbled out of his slacks, nearly tripped onto the bed as he made his way to Eri's embrace.

Eri could feel Hisao's weight on her. They moved in rhythm together.

Then another sound pulled Eri away from the moment. She stopped moving. Her eyes darted around the room. There was nothing out of place. Hisao didn't stop. He continued to brush up against her. His heat consuming her body.

"There it was again," she said.

Hisao groaned in her ear. "It's nothing."

He nuzzled her neck. Eri's worries began to sooth away. Hisao's touch was irresistible. She closed her eyes. She let Hisao do his magic. She could feel his hands exploring her body.

Ecstasy surged through Eri. Hisao was everything she needed at that moment. Her breathing intensified. Nothing else mattered.

Eri moaned, no longer able to control her desires. She opened her eyes.

Then she screamed.

Stan looked down at the two lovers from the bedside.

"Oh, yeah!" Hisao yelled, looking down at Eri.

Stan's blade slammed down onto Eri's face. It burst open her skull. Blood splashed up onto Hisao's eyes. An instant pool formed on the bed.

Hisao pulled away. But it was too late.

Stan struck again. This time his bladed hand cut into Hisao's spine. It ripped through his body and into Eri's stomach.

Hisao tried to escape. His arms clawed at the bed, at Stan's legs. Anything to get him momentum to move. It did no good.

He screamed as Eri's crushed skulled looked up at him. His legs would not move.

Hisao screamed.

The music from the party down the hall drowned out the chance of rescue.

Hisao wanted to tear away from Eri. His mind raced. He needed to move.

Then he felt pressure on the back of his head.

Stan pushed the blunt end of his bladed fist against Hisao's skull and drove him down toward Eri and the bed.

Hisao screamed as his face smashed into the crevice in Eri's head. Blood smeared across his cheeks.

Stan did not relent. He forced Hisao's head down.

Bone began to crack. Hisao's screams were muffled; smothered in the broken face of Eri.

One final crack and Hisao went silent. Blood oozed out of every crevice of his face, mixing with the mess that was once Eri.

The two lovers' heads were one. Hair, skin, blood, and bone all mixed together.

Stan took a step back.

Then he walked away.

Chapter 14

Masaki and Koichi's fingers intertwined as they strolled through the hallway of the apartment complex. Masaki kept close to Koichi. Her arm brushed up against his with every stride. This was the closest she had ever been to him, and she did not want to part ways now.

They didn't speak. Their affection for each other was enough. Their first kiss was the only conversation they needed at the moment.

"Excuse me," were the words that broke Masaki out of her lovesick trance. She looked over to give the attention to the older detective in a trench coat.

Katashi's demeanor showed he didn't care about interrupting Masaki's daydream or the fresh couple's tender moment.

"Have you seen anything strange today?" Katashi asked.

It was a vague question that made Masaki and Koichi share a look of bewilderment.

"I'm Detective Ishida Katashi. I noticed the door at the entrance was broken," continued Katashi. "Have there been any strangers in the apartment building? Anybody you don't recognize?"

"There's an entire party going on," said Koichi. "We don't

recognize half the people here."

"We're celebrating," said Masaki. "It's Coming of Age Day."

"I heard," said Katashi.

"Is there something we should be concerned about?" asked Masaki.

"No," said Katashi, not wanting to project an old man's fears onto their day. "I'm just doing some routine checks. With a party like this, you never know what will happen."

"I'm sure it's all on the up and up," said Koichi with a deeper voice as if imitating a superhero.

"Right," said Katashi with a smirk. "You two have a good day."

"You too," said Masaki.

Then the three of them parted ways. And just like that Masaki's attention was brought back to Koichi by her side. There was nothing to be worried about when she was with him.

Fujiwara Yumiko kept her head down as she navigated through the crowd of party goers. She scrunched her arms in as a way to preserve her kimono. The ceremony may have been over, but she did not want to ruin her dress with a spilled drink. Other guests smiled as Yumiko passed her, but she did not notice. She was focused on finding somebody she knew at the party.

Yumiko brushed by some former classmates. She preferred not to talk to them. She thought she heard her name called out, but it wasn't from a voice she recognized so she ignored it.

After a quick round through the crowded apartment, Yumiko didn't find Masaki or any of her group of friends. Discouraged and overwhelmed, Yumiko made a bee line for the exit.

She took a deep breath once she was out in the hallway. It was much quieter out there, less people around her. A quick glance revealed Masaki was nowhere to be found. Yumiko wondered if Masaki had left all together. Her next stop would have to be Masaki's apartment.

Yumiko started her walk down the hallway. Masaki's apartment was only a few flights away. She could take the stairs.

Katashi wandered through yet another hallway of the Rising Peaks apartment complex. There was more than one party going on. Katashi could hear the hum of music through several walls. Televisions with their volume way up combated the sounds of social activity. In the distance a young woman laughed. Katashi's attention turned to a group down the hall. Four friends were waiting for an elevator. Not a care in the world.

Katashi smirked. Maybe he was wrong. He had jumped to conclusions out of fear and was now on a wild goose chase. He shook his head at his own doubts. His gut feeling wouldn't go away.

Then a scream pulled Katashi's attention back to the elevators. The young woman that was once just laughing was now backing up from the elevator doors with a gasp.

Katashi froze. His hand hovered above his weapon. He was ready to strike.

A shape fumbled out of the elevator. The group of four backed away. Their screams had died down.

Katashi stepped closer. He needed a closer look at what was creeping out of the elevator. The figure was almost seven feet tall. Yellow slimy skin dangled from its body. Two round eyes reflected in the lights as it shuffled out of the elevator.

"Don't go near him!" Katashi yelled. His gun was in his hand. He rushed down the hall to protect the group of friends from the oncoming monster.

"Stay away!" Katashi ordered. He rushed between the group and the monster. His gun was pointed directly at the thing.

Then one of the guys in the group laughed. He pointed at the monster and mocked it.

Katashi could hear the laughter behind him. Finally the moment caught up to him. His brain processed what he was looking at.

It was in fact a kaiju.

But a fake one.

Standing before Katashi was a man in a costume of El Queso Grande, a kaiju from Mexico, formed from a radioactive cheese factory in the 1970's. In his hands was a takeout box of chips and cheese dip. A highlight of every party.

"I'm just going to the party, guy!" the man in the costume yelled. His voice was muffled but Katashi could understand him.

The old detective grimaced. He put his gun away.

The laughter continued behind him. This time it was directed at him and his overzealous actions.

"What are you gonna shoot him for?" asked one of the guys in the group.

"Nothing," said Katashi. He took another looked at the costume of El Queso Grande. The kaiju killed a dozen people in the factory it was formed. It was distasteful to turn it into a party mascot.

"Get going," Katashi dismissed them all with a wave of his arm and a shove of the kaiju costume.

When the coast was clear Katashi once again began to doubt his own thoughts. Maybe Stan wasn't there.

Fujiwara Yumiko was alone now. The hallway had cleared out. She felt more comfortable. Any anxiety the party had given her was gone. But a new one had set in. What if Masaki's parents were home? Should Yumiko go up there and possibly ruin Masaki's plan of ditching the ceremony?

As Yumiko debated her plan, she took the long way around the building. That gave her more time to decide if she wanted to knock on Masaki's door.

The farthest stairwell was just up ahead. Yumiko took slow steps. She wasn't ready to go to Masaki's floor yet.

Just outside the door to the stairwell, Yumiko hesitated. She told herself to just go back to the party. Or go home. She didn't want to get Masaki into any trouble.

Then a sound came from the other side of the door. Footsteps softly echoed in the stairwell.

Yumiko froze. She was tired of dealing with people. She hoped the footsteps would keep going.

They did not.

The footsteps got louder. They were heading for the door Yumiko was directly in front of.

She dropped her head and got out of the way.

The door opened. Yumiko could sense a presence in front of her, but she didn't want to look up. She was going to try to slip by and get into the stairwell. Then the door would close and she would be alone again.

Nobody moved.

Whoever was in Yumiko's way planted their feet at the door. Yumiko was stuck. She looked up just slightly. Two people were holding hands.

"Yumiko!"

Eager arms wrapped around the shy girl.

Masaki squeezed her friend with an encouraging embrace. Koichi stood in the doorway with a smile.

"You made it!" said Masaki. "How was the ceremony?"

"It was okay," said Yumiko, relieved that she had finally found Masaki and she didn't have to go upstairs to do it. "Robotman's video was only few minutes long. I'm not sure if it was even really him."

"I'm so sorry I left you," said Masaki. "I wish you would have come with us."

"I wanted to stay," said Yumiko.

"Have you been to the party yet?" Masaki asked.

"Yes," said Yumiko. "I didn't see anybody there."

"Oh, it's been a little crazy," said Masaki. Her eyes darted to Koichi when she said that. Yumiko saw the gesture and smiled.

"Eri needed to change her clothes," Masaki continued. "I'm not sure where Kayo went."

Yumiko's eyes lit up for a second at the sound of Kayo's name.

"I'll go get some drinks," Koichi volunteered. "You guys go look for Kayo. He probably needs a little cheering up after the scolding Eri gave him."

"What happened?" Yumiko asked.

"He spilled his drink on her," said Masaki. "It's nothing. They'll be fine. You said you didn't see him at all?"

"No," said Yumiko.

"I figured he would have been back by now," said Koichi. "He usually bounces back pretty fast."

"We'll find him," said Masaki. She brushed her hand on Koichi's arm for one last embrace.

"Yumiko, water?" Koichi asked.

"Yes, please," she responded.

Koichi nodded then he stepped away from the two girls.

When he was far enough away from ear shot Yumiko squealed.

"You and Koichi?! What happened?"

"I'll tell you as we look for Kayo," said Masaki.

"Okay," said Yumiko eagerly. She wanted all the details.

Together the two girls practically skipped down the hallway in search of their lost friend. Yumiko was recharged now that she was back with Masaki. And Masaki was happier than ever.

Chapter 15

"Where do you think he could be?" Yumiko asked Masaki as their search for Kayo came up empty. He hadn't returned to the party, and he wasn't in any of the nearby hallways or stairwells. The girls did a quick pass of the nearby floors. Kayo was gone.

"This is all Eri's fault," said Yumiko.

"This isn't her fault," said Masaki. "Kayo is the one who spilled the drink."

"It was an accident," said Yumiko.

Masaki rolled her eyes. Yumiko wasn't even at the party when it happened.

"She should be helping us find him," said Yumiko.

"She won't," said Masaki.

"I don't care," said Yumiko. "Eri is not nice. Why does she have to pick on Kayo like that?"

"Yumiko, Kayo gets himself into that trouble," defended Masaki. "He can be funny, but he's really better in small doses."

"Kayo is funny," said Yumiko. "I wish he'd hang out more with us."

Masaki rolled her eyes again. Then she smiled. Yumiko was looking for the same thing Masaki had just found.

"Eri needs to help us," said Yumiko. "She should apologize

to Kayo."

"We don't even know where Kayo is," said Masaki.

"We'll figure that out," said Yumiko. "With Eri helping we can cover more ground. Maybe Hisao will be there too."

"I really don't think we should drag them into this," said Masaki.

"Yes, we should," said Yumiko, more determined than ever. She broke away from Masaki and headed back for the nearest stairwell. Masaki had no choice but to turn around and join back with her friend.

"Kayo probably found some other friends to hang out with," said Masaki. "He probably left the building."

"He's upset," said Yumiko. "Because of Eri."

They reached Eri's floor. Yumiko stopped along the hallway. She was building up her confidence to confront her friend.

"Don't bother them," said Masaki.

"Why are you defending her?" Yumiko asked.

Masaki hesitated. She didn't want to answer.

"Eri is mean," said Yumiko.

"And I don't want her to be mean to you," said Masaki. "But she's my friend too."

"Why doesn't she like me?" Yumiko asked.

"I don't know," said Masaki. "I wish she did. I wish the three of us could hang out together every day."

"You should stop hanging out with her," Yumiko muttered.

"And she doesn't make me choose sides," Masaki glared.

Yumiko looked to the ground in shame. She regretted her words.

Without thinking, the two girls wound up outside the door of Eri's apartment.

"I'll talk to her," said Masaki. She knocked on the door.

To Masaki's surprise, the door nudged open.

"Oh?" she said as she looked upon the broken lock on the door.

Yumiko paused with fear. She looked over at Masaki, lost at what to do next.

"Eri?" Masaki called out. She pushed the door open further. The apartment was dark. Masaki could hear shuffling, but only shadows graced her vision.

"Anybody home?" Masaki said.

"Were they robbed?" Yumiko asked.

"I don't think so," said Masaki as she laid eyes on the television still in its place.

Masaki took a cautious step forward. Yumiko held on to her friend's arm with a tight grip. The two of them took their steps in unison.

"Eri?" Masaki called out again.

"Turn on the lights," Masaki told Yumiko.

Yumiko reached over and flipped the nearest switch. A bright light shinned in the dining area. The kitchen was empty. The hallway was too long, ending in abysmal darkness.

The couch was untouched in the living room, but the two matching reclining chairs were turned around to face the window.

Masaki stood still. She stared at the two backwards chairs. They always faced the television. Eri's parents were usually found sitting on them watching their favorite shows.

Her eyes trailed each chair until she homed in on the hand that peeked out from the side.

"Eri?" Masaki called out again.

There was no reply.

Masaki stepped forward. She reached out her hand.

"Eri, is that you?"

She placed her hand on the reclining chair. Then with a gentle push, she turned the chair to face her.

Masaki gasped.

Her feet couldn't carry her any faster away from the chair.

There was Kayo. His upper body balanced precariously on top of his lower body. His legs stacked over the other in an unnatural position.

"Kayo!" Yumiko screamed.

Then the other reclining chair shifted. Two bodies slumped onto the floor.

It was the bodies of Eri and Hisao. Their bodies intertwined leading up to their skulls smashed together.

"Oh my God!" Masaki screamed.

Then Eri's body slammed onto the ground. Her broken skull starred up at Masaki and Yumiko. The two girls screamed. Panic had taken over. They stayed frozen in fear, unable to comprehend the idea to run.

A heavy foot step roared from the dark hallway.

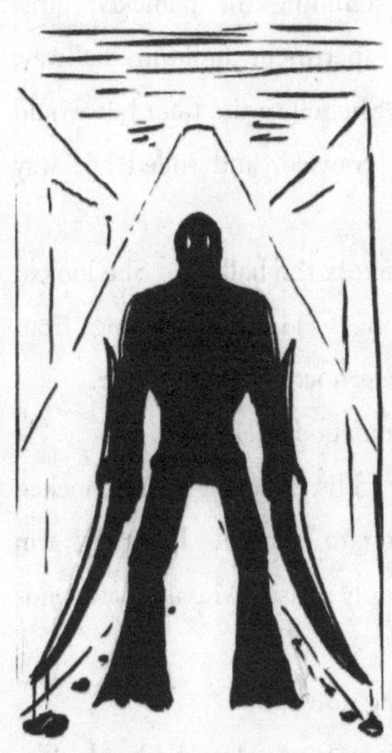

Yumiko, drawn to the noise, turned her body.

That's when they saw him.

Stan stood in the center of the hallway. His breathing raised his chest up and down. His scythe hands were at his side with a body dangling from each one, dripping blood onto the carpet.

As Stan emerged into the light, it was clear who the remaining victims were. Masaki's mother and father.

Masaki screamed.

Stan charged.

A flight response kicked in. Masaki grabbed Yumiko by the shoulders and pushed her toward the exit.

Stan continued the pursuit, dropping the bodies of Masaki's parents in the hallway. There was no haste in his movements. He stepped forward at an inevitable pace.

Masaki and Yumiko slammed into the door at the entryway. Several times Yumiko tried to push the door open. But the door would not budge. She screamed louder than ever, hoping that a neighbor would hear.

Then Masaki pushed her friend aside. She pulled the door open. Light poured in, nearly blinding the panicked girls. Yumiko stumbled out into the apartment building hallway, losing her balance in the process. She fell to the floor but would not stop moving. She shuffled, crawled, and rolled her way further from Stan.

Masaki crashed into the wall across the hallway. She looked back. Stan was still approaching. Heavy breathing from beneath the tentacles of Stan's face echoed in Masaki's ear.

"Help!" Masaki screamed. "Somebody help us!"

Stan stepped out into the light. His imposing figure blocked half of the hallway. He got closer to Masaki. His right arm swiped violently to the floor. He only missed Masaki by seconds as she tried to scurry away.

Then the left arm came crashing down.

It cut into the wall an inch away from Masaki's head. She was forced to stop. Stan had her pinned down. Her eyes followed the right scythe hand as it raised into the air.

Yumiko suddenly tackled Masaki to the ground. Stan's right arm crashed into the wall, tearing away at plaster and wood.

Then a nearby apartment door opened.

A young boy stuck is head out into the hallway, a giant pair of headphones wrapped around his neck.

"Would you be quiet?!" he shouted.

Stan turned his head to look back at the rude young man.

"Jeeezus!" the boy cried out.

Stan charged forward. The boy tried to close his door, but

the tail of his head phones got in the way. The cord dangled in the door's path preventing it from closing.

Stan burst through the door into the boy's hallway. Screams filled the air as the sound of Stan's scythes cracked the building.

Yumiko helped Masaki to her feet. There was no helping the young man. They limped away, wanting to get as much distance as possible from Stan.

Their cries for help went unnoticed.

Stan stepped back out into the hallway. His latest kill finished.

Masaki and Yumiko did not stop. They hurried as fast as their fear could take them. They entered the stairwell. It was a clear path to the exit, only fourteen floors down. But Masaki suddenly stopped. She took a deep breath while Yumiko urged her to move.

But Masaki wouldn't budge.

"Koichi is at the party," said Masaki. "We have to get him."

"We have to get out," said Yumiko.

"I can't leave him," said Masaki.

Yumiko looked at the stairwell going down. Then she looked at Masaki. "We have to leave him."

"No," said Masaki. "Please."

Yumiko hesitated. She eyed her path to salvation. Then she looked back at Masaki.

"Please," Masaki said again.

"Let's go get Koichi," Yumiko agreed.

United once again, Masaki and Yumiko rushed out of the

stairwell.

There was no fear down the hallway. Party goers continued to enjoy the day as if nothing was happening.

That all changed when Masaki and Yumiko burst through the door. They screamed at the top of their lungs.

"Run!" Masaki yelled. "Run! Get out of here! There's a monster!"

Most of the party goers looked at the two girls with questionable glances. But others took their words to more heart.

It wasn't long before the message spread and panic flooded the area. People started running for the nearest exit. The elevators were jammed packed, stairwells echoed with the sound of footsteps.

Then Detective Ishida Katashi appeared.

"What's going on?" he cried out. Masaki collapsed at the detective's feet. The mirage of safety was all that she needed to finally rest.

"Are you okay?" he asked, bending a knee to get closer to Masaki.

"I think so," she said.

"What happened?" asked Katashi. "What's going on?"

Masaki shook her head. She couldn't put it into words what she had seen.

"We have to run," is what she got out. "It's going to kill us!"

Chapter 16

"Where did you see it?" Katashi had asked.

This simple phrase sent the detective and the two scared girls back down the hallway toward Eri's apartment and the monster that now resided there.

The floor was abuzz with whispers. Some had left thanks to Masaki's pleas. Others remained close to the walls, unsure of their next move. Could the party restart? Should they leave? Many wanted to wait it out.

The hallway was eerily quiet. Katashi had his gun at the ready. He wasn't sure what he would find, but Stan or not, the girls were scared of something.

"Here," said Masaki, returning to Eri's front door. "It was in there. They're all in there…"

Masaki's voice broke away. She didn't want to face the reality. Her friends were dead. Her family. What was there left?

Katashi looked down both ends of the hallway. The coast was clear.

"Stay here," he ordered the two girls. "I'm going to check it out. If it comes back, I want you to scream. Let everyone know. And run. Don't wait for me."

Yumiko nodded at Katashi's instructions. She didn't have to be told twice to run away.

"What if he's in there?" Masaki asked.

Katashi stopped. He took in a deep breath as if giving himself time to formulate a plan in case Masaki was right.

"You'll hear the gun shots," he said. "Don't wait for me."

Masaki nodded.

Katashi opened the door to the apartment. Masaki couldn't help herself. She looked inside. Eri's dead body was in clear view. Masaki winced, angry at herself for stealing one last look.

Katashi gave a glance around then he walked into the apartment, leaving the two girls alone in the hallway.

"We need to get out of here," said Yumiko.

Masaki shook her head. "I need to find Koichi. We need to stay with the detective."

Yumiko was on the balls of her feet. She was ready to flee at a moment's notice. "What if it's still in there? What if it kills him and we don't know it?"

"He'll warn us," said Masaki with certainty.

"He could be dead already," said Yumiko.

Masaki turned to the apartment door. She cracked the door open just a little. But the gap didn't matter, Masaki's eyes focused on Eri's dead body like it did before. She wanted to close her eyes, but she couldn't. She couldn't let her guard down.

"Is everything okay in there?" Masaki called out with a whisper to Katashi.

There was silence.

"Are you there?" Masaki called out.

The darkened apartment did not respond. Eri's busted face stared at Masaki.

"Please, come back!" Yumiko called out. "Please!"

"Shhhh," Masaki shut up her friend. "Don't be so loud. And he doesn't need to come back. We're fine."

"You don't know that!" Yumiko cried. "We need to just go."

"We need to help," said Masaki.

"Then you help," said Yumiko. "I'm leaving. He's dead."

"Don't go," said Masaki.

Then Masaki moved against her better judgment. She swung the apartment door open. Light poured in from the hallway. The three bodies of her friends were clear as day. Masaki rushed in. She turned her back to the death that filled the room.

"Detective!" she screamed. "Are you there?"

Masaki froze. She heard the shuffling of footsteps come from the dark hallway that she saw Stan come from earlier. The hallway with her parents.

The shadows moved.

Regret filled Masaki's gut. Every thought in her mind told her to run, but her body could not do it.

Then Katashi came out of the shadows of the hallway.

"What are you doing in here?" he asked. "I told you to wait out there."

"Yumiko was getting worried," she said.

"It's clear," said Katashi. "There's nothing here. Just bodies."

"Yeah…" said Masaki, once again reminded of everything she had lost that day.

"Did you know them?" Katashi asked, sensing Masaki's misfortune.

Tears welled up in her eyes. She nodded her head, unable to say the words.

Then a scream broke from the hallway.

Masaki would have to bury her pain a little longer.

"It's back!" Yumiko shouted.

Katashi and Masaki shared a look of shock. Then they ran out to the hallway.

Yumiko was frozen in fear. She didn't budge even as Katashi and Masaki ran up to her side. Her stare was off in the distance.

And for good reason. Stan stood at the end of the hallway, blood dripping from his scythe hands.

"Run," said Katashi. "Get out of the building."

"What about everybody else?" Masaki asked.

"Get them out," said Katashi. "Get everybody out!"

Katashi stepped forward. His gun came up. It pointed directly at the motionless Stan.

"Put your hands up!" Katashi shouted at Stan.

Stan did not comply. The murderer tilted its head, examining Katashi.

Katashi did not hesitate. He fired his gun.

The first shout echoed through the hallway. It was a direct hit. Stan shook from the impact. But the monster did not drop.

Katashi fired several more shots straight into the chest of Stan.

The blows proved devastating. Stan rocked back and forth. On the last shot, the monster collapsed, sprawling on to the floor on its back.

Katashi froze. His gun was still aimed at Stan. He waited. Stan did not move. It wasn't until several more moments did Katashi feel safe.

Stan wasn't moving.

Stan was dead.

Katashi breathed a sigh of relief.

A commotion stirred in the apartment complex. It was easy to ignore two girls screaming for help, but the sound of gunshots was a good call to retreat.

Heads poked out of doorways. Questions repeated over and over again. Everybody wanted to know what was going on.

They all wanted answers from Katashi. Each voice competed with another, despite them all wanting the same information.

"Please, evacuate the building," Katashi yelled. "I want everybody off of this floor! This is the police. This building is under an evacuation."

Then Katashi pulled the fire alarm.

Lights strobed as the alarm screeched in everybody's ear. That was the straw that broke the camel's back. Residents rushed out of their apartments looking to save themselves from the threatened fire.

"Move this way, people!" Katashi shouted, gesturing with wide arms for people to follow him away from Stan's body.

"To the north side of the building!" Katashi instructed. "Keep away from the body!"

Masaki and Yumiko remained where they were. Masaki did not want to leave the safety of Katashi. Thanks to him this nightmare was over.

Then Stan sat up.

Masaki's eyes widened with fear. She gasped. Katashi had not seen it yet. She watched in horror as Stan got back to his feet.

"It's alive!" Masaki screamed.

Katashi, busy directing the crowd, finally turned around. His confidence dropped. Stan stood as strong as ever.

"How?" he wondered out loud to himself.

Suddenly, Katashi knew he was past his jurisdiction. He had been right. But he was the only one that could help now.

"Move!" Katashi yelled with renewed vigor. "Keep away from it!"

Stan stepped forward.

Katashi's stomach dropped. He had failed.

The hallway was too tight. Bodies were shoulder to shoulder, trying to run away from the fire, many unaware of the real dangers behind them.

Stan approached the congested crowd. His arms swung high into the air.

Then they came crashing down into the flesh and bones of his latest victims.

Retreat was not an option.

Screams filled the hallway. Blood splashed against the walls and the ceiling. There was no place to run for many of the residents. They were stuck to face the blade of Stan or get crushed by the stampede of their neighbors trying to escape.

"We have to go!" Katashi said to Masaki and Yumiko. He took their hands and forced them to their feet. The three of them moved with the crowd. Stan was a way away, blocked by the climbing number of bodies on the floor.

The stairwell was blocked. The elevators were packed and gone from their floor. There was no place left to run.

"Back into your apartments!" Katashi shouted. "Everybody, get inside an apartment and hide. Do not open the door for anybody!"

Katashi held his grip on the two girls. They rushed through

the apartment complex, away from Stan.

Then Masaki stopped.

Katashi was nearly taken off his feet. He was not expecting Masaki to break away like that.

"We have to go," said Katashi.

"No," said Masaki.

"What are you doing?" he asked.

"In here," said Masaki.

She was staring at the door to Koichi's apartment.

"We'll hide in here," she said again.

Katashi shrugged. He stepped forward and opened the door.

Yumiko rushed in. Masaki was right behind her.

Katashi slammed the door behind them.

They were safe for now.

"Masaki!"

Masaki looked over. Her worries melted away from her for the moment.

Koichi rushed up to her and threw his arms around her. They embraced, never wanting to let go of each other again.

"You're alright!" Masaki shouted.

"I was so worried," said Koichi.

"I wasn't going to leave without you," said Masaki. "I would never leave you."

"And I'd never leave you," said Koichi.

Katashi rolled his eyes at the young love. He didn't have time to deal with pleasantries. He dragged the living room couch over to the front entrance of the apartment, securing it against the door.

Stan may have been able to take several bullets, but he would have a challenge getting through the door.

"Somebody call the police," said Katashi. "We're staying here until back up arrives. Do you have any kind of weapons?"

"No," Koichi shook his head.

"Then find whatever you can," said Katashi. "Blunt objects, kitchen knives. Anything to defend yourself."

"Can we fight that thing out there?" Masaki asked.

Katashi shook his head. "I don't know."

Chapter 17

"Do you hear anything?" Koichi asked Katashi, guarding the door of the apartment. The once lively party was over. The room was silent with held breaths as if any noise would alert Stan to their presence.

Cautiously, Katashi slid to the center of the door where the peep hole was. He looked at the warped hallway through the small bit of glass.

Stan was nowhere to be found.

"He's gone," said Katashi.

"Then let's get out of here," said Yumiko.

"No," said Katashi. "Not yet. We have to wait for back up."

"We shouldn't be here," cried Yumiko. "I shouldn't have come to this party. I should have stayed home."

Masaki wrapped her arms around her distraught friend. Yumiko shrugged off the embrace. "You trapped me here," she said through emerging tears.

Masaki didn't say anything. She leaned back over to Koichi. He adjusted so she could let her head rest on his shoulder. Yumiko scoffed at the sight.

"So what do we do?" Koichi asked.

"I'll go out there," said Katashi.

"No," said Masaki. "You can't."

"We need to get eyes on Stan," argued Katashi. "If we can find him we can maneuver around him."

"What about us?" Yumiko asked.

"Stay here," said Katashi. "And do not open the door for anything until I come back."

"What if that thing returns?" Koichi asked.

"I won't be far," said Katashi. "I'll know."

"And if you don't?" Yumiko butted in.

"Keep the door barricaded," said Katashi. "If I can find Stan then when help arrives we'll be able to swarm the monster and handle the situation."

"We're all going to die…" Yumiko let out.

"You're not going to die," said Katashi. He shifted the couch a foot away from the door. "When I'm out, put this couch back into place. Immediately."

Koichi nodded his head.

Katashi took a breath.

"Don't do anything stupid," said Katashi. "Help will be here soon. Until then, nobody opens that door. Do not go anywhere."

Heads nodded in the room.

Then Katashi cracked open the apartment door and slipped through back to the hallway.

Across the hallway on the fourteenth floor, elevator doors opened. A group of four young adults walked out of the small compartment. The two guys' suits draped around their bodies. Their shirts were untucked, and jackets hung loosely. One had his tie wrapped around his head like a headband. The two girls with them were still in their kimonos from an earlier Coming of Age ceremony.

They were adults now. It was time to party.

"Where's the party at?" one of the girls asked when they arrived to a quiet hallway.

"14D!" mumbled her drunken boyfriend. He adjusted his tie headband and pointed in the proper direction down the hallway.

"Are you sure? I don't hear anything."

"Thick walls," he replied.

The group of four stumbled through the hallway. They passed several doors, not noticing the cracks on the frames and dented hinges.

Stan slipped out of a broken doorway, silent compared to the two couples stumbling through the hallway looking for the party.

Their footsteps were hard against the thin carpet of the apartment building. As they walked forward they didn't notice the sound of the fifth pair of footsteps walking slowly behind them.

Masaki and Koichi huddled against the wall of the apartment near the front entrance. Yumiko sat on the far side of the area near the balcony. She stared down at her feet, rocking back and forth.

Masaki stood up. She wanted to comfort her friend, even if Yumiko didn't want it.

Yumiko shifted to look away from Masaki on her approach. That did not stop Masaki. When she was close, Masaki leaned down to talk to her face to face.

"It's going to be okay," Masaki assured Yumiko.

"No, it's not," said Yumiko. "Our friends are dead. Your parents are dead."

Masaki got quiet. It was a truth she didn't want to face yet.

"We're still alive," said Masaki. "We'll make it through this."

"We're all going to die," said Yumiko.

"Shut up!" Koichi shouted, overhearing the two girls' conversation. "Shut up! What is your problem?"

"We're trapped at a party with a monster outside!" Yumiko shouted back. "It's going to kill us!"

"We can wait this out," said Koichi.

"If we wait here we are all going to die," said Yumiko.

"That's not true," said Masaki.

"What, is Koichi going to protect you?" Yumiko snarled.

Masaki gasped. She had never heard Yumiko's voice get as venomous as it did.

"What's wrong with Koichi?" Masaki asked.

Yumiko remained silent.

The two girls looked at each other. Unsure of where their friendship now lied.

Then the screaming started.

The sound erupted from the hallway outside of the

apartment. Everybody stared at the door that separated them from certain death. It felt like a thin piece of wood was all that protected them.

The screams quickly died away.

Masaki took in another breath. Whoever had been out there was now dead. Killed by the hands of a monster.

"Maybe they got away," said Koichi.

"They're dead," said Yumiko.

"Don't say that," said Masaki.

"They're dead," Yumiko repeated.

Then another scream filled the hallway. Closer than ever.

Koichi jumped to his feet, sensing the coming danger.

He rushed to the door to get a peek through the peephole.

"There's somebody out there!" he shouted. "Oh my god, it's Madoka."

Out in the hallway, the young man with the tie around his forehead, and school mate of Koichi, crawled on his hands and knees. Blood covered his already messy suit. A trail of blood stained the carpet behind him.

"What do we do?" Koichi asked. "Can we help him?"

"We're not supposed to open the door," Masaki said hesitantly.

"I don't see the thing," said Koichi.

"We can't open the door," said Masaki.

"We need to run," said Yumiko. "We can't stay here."

"Where is Katashi?" Masaki asked.

"I don't see him either," said Koichi. "We need to help

Madoka."

Madoka's screams grew louder. He pleaded for help in the empty hallway.

"We can't leave him out there," said Koichi.

"Please don't go," said Masaki.

"I'll be quick," justified Koichi. "I'll run out there, grab him, and be back in just like that."

"Don't do it," Masaki said softly.

"The coast is clear," said Koichi. "I have to."

Then he turned away from his new girlfriend and cracked open the door to the apartment. The pleas of Madoka were even louder now.

Masaki rushed to the front door as Koichi began his trek through the hallway. She did not close the door. Instead, she stayed at the ready watching over Koichi.

"Help me!" Madoka screamed.

Koichi rushed up to his suffering friend, Madoka. Madoka reached up toward Koichi, looking for any bit of help. Blood quickly got onto Koichi's clothes and arms.

"Come on," Koichi said. "Can you get to your feet?"

Madoka stumbled. He was too weak. He had gashes across his legs preventing him from standing up.

"I've got you," said Koichi. He grabbed Madoka from behind and began to drag his schoolmate toward the apartment.

Little did he know it was a trap.

Masaki screamed. "He's here!"

Stan emerged from a nearby doorway. The silent juggernaut

did not hesitate. His right arm swiped across the air. It was only inches away from Koichi.

Koichi yelled. He let go of Madoka and stumbled backward. He could see Masaki at the open apartment door in the corner of his eye. His feet kept him scooting away from Stan. Another swipe of the bladed hand came crashing down, scraping against Koichi's foot.

"Get inside!" Koichi warned Masaki. "Close the door!"

"Noooo," Masaki yelled.

But it was too late.

Stan lunged forward. Both his arms crashed down where Koichi lay. The boney blades cut through Koichi's stomach, straight into the floor.

Blood erupted from Koichi's mouth. Crimson red stained the rest of his clothes, some from Madoka, but most from himself now.

And Stan did not stop there. With his blades securely in Koichi, he spread his arms wide, tearing through the sides of his victim and eventually ripping Koichi's body in half.

Masaki screamed. Try as she might, she couldn't close her eyes. She watched as her boyfriend was torn into pieces across the hallway floor.

Stan stared down the hallway at Masaki. His head tilted, once again examining his target.

No longer thinking clearly, Masaki retreated away from the door, forgoing the open entrance or barricading the entryway with the couch.

Stan stood up straight. He remained still for a moment then shifted back around. He stared down at Madoka.

Madoka gargled blood, fighting to crawl away.

It did no good.

Stan stepped down on Madoka preventing his latest victim from moving. A blade came down to the side of Madoka's head. He tried to scream with a mouthful of blood. Madoka squirmed, but discovered his head was stuck. Stan had snagged the tail of his tie. It was tight against his skull, keeping his head and neck propped up.

Then Stan's second blade sliced across Madoka's exposed neck.

Blood gushed out of Madoka's head, draining the color from his face. He fell dead to the floor.

Stan stood back up. He turned around. It was time to turn his sights back on the two girls.

Masaki scurried around the room. She rushed to the kitchen and grabbed the biggest knife she could find. Meanwhile, Yumiko huddled in the corner of the living room. In her scared mind it was the safest place in the room, far away from the entrance.

"Yumiko!" Masaki shouted when coming back to the living room with her chef's knife. "You need to get up!"

Yumiko shook her head. "We'regoingtodiewe'regoingtodie…" she repeated over and over again.

Masaki stood guard over Yumiko. "No, we're not."

The door to the apartment crumbled.

Stan slammed his blades against the cheap wood. Splinters rained across the room.

The couch was little of an obstacle. Stan forced his way through the entryway. He was an unstoppable machine.

Masaki put a tighter grip on her knife. She rushed forward once Stan was visible in the living room. The knife was held high, ready to strike.

Stan swiped his arm, knocking Masaki to the side. She crashed into the wall, dropping her knife in the process.

Stan took another step toward Yumiko.

There was nowhere to run. Yumiko was trapped in the corner of the apartment.

Stan raised his arms, ready to make his kill.

Then gun shots echoed in the room.

Stan staggered on his feet. Two more gun shots roared, drawing Stan's attention away from Yumiko for a moment.

Katashi stood at the destroyed doorway, gun in hand.

"Run!" Katashi ordered.

Masaki scrambled to her feet, but Yumiko did not move.

Stan shifted in the center of the living room. Katashi fired one more shot. And that was all he had left.

His gun clicked with nothing in the chamber. Stan tilted his head. He looked back and forth from Katashi to Yumiko.

"Stan!" Katashi yelled. "Over here!"

Stan looked at Katashi for several moments, as if seeing him for the first time.

"That's right," said Katashi. "I know who you are. I remember you."

As Katashi distracted Stan, Masaki rushed over to Yumiko on the other side of the apartment.

"We have to go," she whispered to her friend. "Come on, get up. We have to run."

Yumiko shook her head. She was too afraid.

"Please, Yumiko!" Masaki begged. She tried to pull Yumiko to her feet, but Yumiko would not budge.

Stan remained where he was, looking over at Katashi.

"How many have you killed, Stan?" Katashi asked. "I saw what you did to that family. Were there more before that? How many before?"

Stan was silent.

Then the monster turned his back to Katashi.

"No!" Katashi shouted. He tried to fire his empty weapon again. Then out of desperation he threw his gun at Stan. It merely hit the monster in the back and fell to the ground with little punishment.

Stan returned to his crusade for Yumiko.

"Yumiko!" Masaki screamed.

Finally, Yumiko jumped to her feet. Masaki was nearly blindsided by her actions.

But Yumiko did not run for the exit. She headed the opposite direction for the balcony.

"No, Yumiko!" Masaki shouted. She reached out for her friend but it was too late. Yumiko rushed outside to the balcony, fourteen floors above the street.

Desperately, Masaki followed. She grabbed Yumiko's arm to pull her back inside, but Stan was on them. The monster had them cornered on the balcony.

Masaki rushed to the edge of the balcony. She looked down. There was no surviving that fall. Her mind raced. Could they jump to another balcony?

Stan walked into the window doorway, shattering the glass with his mere physicality.

Masaki and Yumiko screamed. There was no where left to run.

Stan stood out on the balcony. The wind roared around him. He had the girls pinned down. His blades rose into the air like fangs in a wild animal.

But Katashi had other plans.

The older detective slammed into Stan.

He put as much force into the blow as he could, driving his shoulder into the spine of the monster.

Stan was knocked off balance. The wind rushed by.

Katashi kept the pressure on. He shoved Stan closer to the ledge.

Stan stumbled. A wild swing of his arm pierced Katashi in the leg.

Then Stan folded over the balcony's ledge. His bladed hands hung low throwing the weight of his body over the edge.

Stan's feet left the floor.

And just like that Stan slipped out into the air.

Gravity took hold, pulling Stan down toward the streets below.

Katashi watched as Stan got smaller. Then the massive body of the monster crashed into the pavement, cratering through the ground and into the dark abyss below the city.

Katashi exhaled. His body went limp. He collapsed to his knees with only the ledge able to prop him up.

Masaki and Yumiko stared at Katashi, their savior.

Together the three of them sat in blissful silence.

They were no longer in danger.

"Is it over?" Masaki asked.

Katashi nodded. "He's gone."

"Who was that?" she asked.

"A bad man," said Katashi. "Fueled by hate."

"He killed my family," said Masaki. "My friends."

"Because you were loved," said Katashi.

None of the three tried to move. They were content where they were. The sounds of sirens echoed below.

Katashi smiled. Back up had finally arrived.

Chapter 18

Smoke rose from the cracks that webbed across the broken street. Police cars, ambulances, fire trucks, and more had swarmed the area. Bright lights twirled in the afternoon shadows of Tokyo. A distraught crowd piled up along the sidewalks outside of the apartment complex. Everybody wanted a peek at the aftermath of Stan's murder spree.

Gurneys with body bags filtered out of the building one after the other. Each attendant that hurried out of the building shared the same grim expression. This was something that nobody should have to see.

Masaki and Yumiko sat together on the edge of an ambulance. Blankets hung over their shoulders, offering a warm layer of security.

"He was coming after me," Yumiko remorsed. "Why was he coming after me?"

"I don't know," Masaki tried to offer as comfort. She knew it would do no good, but it was the only answer she had.

Masaki's eyes stayed on the hole that Stan had formed when he went crashing through the street. Several rescue officers had propelled down into the dark abyss to pull up the body of the vengeful monster. She waited to see the dead body of her tormentor. The monster had taken everything away from her. Seeing his remains was the least she could get.

"How are you two doing?" Katashi came up, interrupting Masaki's concentration.

"Is it dead?" Yumiko asked.

"Yes," said Katashi. "It's over. Nothing is surviving that fall."

"It wasn't nothing," said Masaki.

Katashi knelt down. He looked Masaki in the eye.

"Stan was a terrible old man," said Katashi. "That anger fueled his rampage, but he's done. You don't have to be afraid anymore."

Masaki lowered her eyes. She couldn't help it. She was afraid. Everything had changed that day. There was nothing left but fear for what the future would bring.

"I understand your parents were two of the victims," said Katashi with a hushed voice.

Tears welled up in Masaki's eyes. She had been holding back the fact of her murdered parents since laying eyes on them. She was not yet ready to face that.

"I've put in a call to foster services," said Katashi. "It wouldn't be anything official. I have friends there that can help point you in the right direction."

Masaki did not move. If she acknowledged Katashi's words then that would make her parents' death a truth in her mind.

"Do you have a place you can go to for now?" Katashi asked.

Masaki finally looked up at Katashi.

She shook her head.

Her whole life was at the apartment. Her family. Her friends.

All of that was torn away.

"I will take care of you," offered Katashi.

Masaki began to smile.

Then the earth rumbled.

The street pulsated under everybody's feet. Windows shattered from the pressure as buildings swayed in the air. People screamed as they tried to run for cover.

More cracks erupted in the pavement. Thunder roared from the scar in the road. From the dark abyss, more screams echoed out from the rescuers down below.

Katashi grabbed hold of both Masaki and Yumiko. He pulled them out of the ambulance they were resting in. The thunder continued. The force of the sound could be felt coming from underneath the city.

"What is that?" Masaki asked.

Her question was answered right away.

The street erupted. Concrete and debris flew into the air.

The ambulance the three were just at flipped onto its side.

And a familiar sight shot out of the ground.

Stan's bone scythe hand rose into the air, only this time it was thirty meters long.

The massive object ascended into the sky as more of Stan climbed out of its dark hell. The second hand broke through the surface a block away. Dozens of unlucky people were crushed by the debris or fell into the black abyss that Stan was emerging from.

Stan's head was the size of a bus. Dust shook from its tentacled mouth as it embraced the sun again.

It only took a matter of seconds, but Tokyo now was under the shadow of a kaiju.

Stan stood tall with the skyscrapers of the Japanese city. Its feet brushed up against the police cars and ambulances in the area. Like ants, people squirmed away from its presence. Stan took a step, crushing several people in the process. But the kaiju's attention was focused. Then the monster found its target.

Masaki and Yumiko screamed. Stan was looking right at them.

"Get them out of here!" Katashi yelled. He tightened his grip around the girls' arms and forced them to run.

Stan shifted on his feet. He began his methodical trek

toward his prey.

Katashi signaled for other officials to get in their cars. He rushed the girls over to the closest vehicle. Stan took another step, sending people to the ground.

Katashi opened the door of the back seat. "Get in!"

He forced Yumiko into the car. Then shut the door behind her.

With a slap of the roof, Katashi signal for the driver to go.

"Wait! Yumiko!" Masaki yelled.

"Masaki!" Yumiko screamed through the car's window. She pounded on the glass as the car sped off.

Katashi did not stop. He hurried Masaki along. Another car was nearby. Just like Yumiko, he shoved Masaki into the back seat of the car. Then Katashi jumped into the driver's seat.

Stan took another step. Its foot brushed against Katashi's car, stepping where the two of them were standing just moments ago.

Masaki screamed.

Katashi's foot slammed down on the gas pedal.

The car sped off, away from the towering Stan.

Stan paused. The kaiju tilted its head as it watched both cars tear away through Tokyo.

Katashi was quick. His car caught up with Yumiko's in less than a minute. Masaki looked out her window. She could see Yumiko scream back at her friend. Yumiko slammed her fists against the window. Her voice could not be heard, but her face told the story. She was crying for help from her friend. Masaki rushed up against the window of the car. She wanted to reach out. She wanted to protect Yumiko from being hurt any more.

Stan followed closely by. The kaiju advanced with ease with every step it took. Buildings crumbled around the monster as its scythe hands collided with the structures around it.

Katashi watched Stan through the rearview mirror. The kaiju was surprisingly fast. It was going to be on top of them shortly if they didn't do anything.

An intersection was up ahead. Cars had already stopped, congesting the area. Drivers ran from their vehicles at the sight of Stan on its way.

Katashi took the opportunity to make space between him and Yumiko's car. Stan would have to make a choice on whom to follow. It would save at least one life.

The two cars separated. Masaki cried out for Yumiko as she grew smaller in the distance.

Stan was nearly on top of them. The kaiju looked down at its prey.

Suddenly, Yumiko's car stopped.

Masaki watched in horror. The car was blocked in the intersection. Abandoned cars littered the area. There was no place to go.

Masaki screamed. For a moment she made eye contact with Yumiko.

Stan raised its scythe arm high into the air.

Masaki froze. Her car kept driving away. But her focus was entirely on Yumiko in her last moments.

Stan's boney blade drove into Yumiko's car.

Metal twisted, windows shattered, and bones broke. The car exploded from the pressure of Stan's attack as Yumiko screamed one final time.

Dust and debris filled the streets. Masaki cried as her friend was lost to the chaos.

Stan stepped forward. Its blade rose back up into the air. A victorious roar rumbled across Tokyo.

Now, all eyes were on Masaki.

"Hang on," said Katashi. He pushed the car to its limits.

Stan stomped down just missing the vehicle.

Katashi jerked the wheel. The street was becoming unstable. He weaved through several stopped cars.

A tunnel was up ahead. Katashi smirked. If he could reach the tunnel they might have a chance to break away. He kept his focus on the street ahead. Stan remained close behind. Masaki could not look away. Her neck craned up as she stared down Stan walking behind them.

Just another half mile. Katashi took in a deep breath. He could make it.

The car sped along the street with Stan on its tail.

A bladed bone struck the street, landing where the car was just at a second ago. Then Stan's second scythe hand snapped forward. Katashi saw it coming out of the corner of his eye. He swerved to dodge the attack at the last second.

The car spun out of control as the tires squealed. Stan ripped its blade out of the street and pushed forward. Katashi regained control of the car. The opening of the tunnel beckoned him.

Stan got back to its feet. Its arms were rising once again.

The unrelenting fate of Stan loomed overhead.

More cars were left abandoned at the entrance of the tunnel. Katashi did a quick scan as he raced forward to salvation. There was an opening on the opposite street. But it was short. He would have to make a sharp turn and hope for the best once he got in the tunnel. There was no telling what was hiding just beyond the shadows.

Katashi said a small prayer and drifted into his new path. It took him closer to Stan than he would have preferred.

The kaiju paused as Katashi drove past the monster's feet. Stan roared, insulted by Katashi's hubris.

Katashi paid no attention. He kept his sights on the narrow entrance allowed for him to enter the tunnel. He picked up the pace. The street was clear. All he had to do was hurry.

Stan stepped forward. The kaiju's long stride carried it closer to the tunnel's entrance. Katashi cursed as he watched Stan raise its scythes.

Katashi gritted his teeth. There was nowhere else to go. He and Masaki were on a collision course with either the tunnel or Stan's blade.

Masaki was quiet. Her fear had vanished. Wiped away by vengeance.

Stan's blade came crashing down.

Katashi drifted to the side at the final moment. Stan's blade cut across the right side of the car. The frame cracked. Glass shattered, sprinkling onto the passengers. The street erupted, flipping the vehicle into the tunnel.

Over and over the car flipped with Katashi and Masaki inside. It slammed against several cars before stopping, back on its wheels, over a dozen meters into temporary salvation.

Stan roared. Thunderous slams could be felt all around the tunnel. Stan was striking out at the structure that was protecting its latest victims.

Masaki teetered in her seat. Glass hung from her hair. Tiny cuts graced her face, though she wouldn't have known. There was no pain at that moment. There was only survival.

Katashi leaned up against the bent door frame. Blood gushed out of a wound on his forehead. His breathing was shallow.

"Katashi?" Masaki whispered. "Katashi, are you okay?"

Katashi answered with a groan. His hands shook as he tried to raise them back to the steering wheel. They only moved a few inches before dropping back down to his lap.

Another crash echoed in the tunnel. Stan would not relent.

"We have to go," said Masaki. "We have to get out of here."

Katashi moaned again. He nodded his head in agreement but made no move to advance.

"Go," said Katashi.

"What about you?" Masaki asked.

"I'll be fine," said Katashi.

"I'm not leaving you," said Masaki.

"You have to," Katashi said weakly, waving her off.

Stan's pursuit of Masaki continued. The thirty-meter blade of his hand crashed against the entrance of the tunnel. It was too long to strike from the inside. The walls reverberated all around them. Dust and debris fell from the ceiling.

"It can't reach us," said Masaki over the sound of the tunnel slowly crumbling around them in a rain of pebbles. "It's can't reach us."

"Go," Katashi said again. "I'll catch up in a minute."

"I go when you go," said Masaki, not budging on her decision.

Katashi nodded. He accepted her choice with a smile.

"I'll be good in a moment. Just let me catch my breath," he said in a hushed tone.

Then another rumble echoed in the distance.

The attack on the tunnel ceased.

Silence overtook the tunnel. The only sound that remained was the thunderous footsteps coming from the distance.

"What is that?" Masaki asked. "What's coming?"

Katashi smiled.

He knew the sound of those footsteps.

Help was on the way.

Outside of the tunnel, Stan stood tall. Its attention was on a newcomer, emerging from the outskirts of Tokyo.

Standing just a mile away was a new adversary.

Robotman was ready to protect the people of Tokyo from the kaiju threat.

Punch!

Punch!

Punch!

Chapter 19

Stan stood its ground. The unstoppable kaiju looked on at its newest challenge standing just a few meters shorter, the mecha-protector of Asia, Robotman.

Metal armor glistened in the sunlight. Robotman stretched out its arms, performing motions of a wushu attack, set to intimidate the kaiju threat of Stan. Air whooshed against the robot's movements.

"Robotman is here!" Masaki cried out. She could see his feet from the car in the tunnel. The mech was standing between them and the threat of Stan.

"About time," said Katashi with a gargled voice.

Outside, Stan stared back at Robotman. The menacing presence of the kaiju was unimpressed with Robotman's ability.

Robotman rushed forward. The mech jumped into the air. A swift kick struck Stan across the chest. Stan stumbled back several steps, but the monster did not fall.

Robotman circled around. The mech delivered several more strikes with its feet. Stan staggered. Then Robotman swooped in with a powerful left hook across Stan's slimy chin. The punch rattled the skull of the kaiju, knocking the monster back into several buildings.

"It's doing it!" Masaki yelled. "It's beating Stan!"

Katashi readjusted in his seat. He could only see a fraction of the fight from his vantage point. He turned and glanced deeper into the tunnel. There were dozens of abandoned cars, but there was a path. At least, a path that got them further away from Stan.

Katashi lifted his hand toward the ignition. The keys dangled just a few inches away from him.

"We need to get out of here," said Katashi. "We need to keep running."

He turned the keys in the ignition. The engine refused to turn on. Katashi twisted the keys several times with nothing changing.

"Damn it!" Katashi screamed.

"What do we do?" Masaki asked.

"It wants to turn on," said Katashi. He reached for the keys again.

This time with a little prayer, he turned the keys.

The engine roared to life.

Masaki screamed with glee. Katashi laughed. They were still in the game.

"We're okay," he reassured Masaki. "We're going to be okay."

Debris filled the streets. Smoke and dust took to the air. Stan was somewhere, hidden in the smoke. Robotman squared up once again, waiting to see its opponent.

Stan rushed forward out of the veil of debris. The kaiju hacked away toward Robotman with its scythes. Surprised by the sudden speed of Stan, Robotman was struck by two of Stan's blows. Bone scraped against metal. Sparks shot out of Robotman's wounds.

The mech rebounded. It back flipped out of Stan's range of attack. Robotman performed several motions and was ready for another round.

Stan paced forward. Robotman followed the back-and-forth motion, constantly taking a step back to keep its range far enough away from Stan's scythes.

The scythes lashed out several more times. Ready this time, Robotman dodged the attacks.

Then Robotman retaliated. A flurry of kicks and punches struck Stan. Knees dug into Stan's gut, fists and feet pounded against Stan's head. Robotman was landing every strike with pinpoint accuracy.

Stan stumbled. The kaiju staggered on its feet. Another blow from Robotman hit Stan square on the chest, sending the kaiju down to the ground.

The ground rumbled inside of the tunnel. The car shook violently. More debris fell from the ceiling.

"Let's go!" Masaki yelled.

Katashi nodded. They had rested long enough.

He pushed down on the gas pedal.

But the car did not move.

Katashi pushed down again.

Nothing.

"What's wrong?" Masaki asked. "What's going on?"

"I can't…," said Katashi. "I can't move my feet."

"What?"

"I can't feel my legs," he realized.

"No!" Masaki cried.

"We're not going anywhere," Katashi admitted.

"No," said Masaki again. She shifted in the backseat of the car. With force she was able to bust the back door open. Dust and debris spilled over her as she exited the car. "We have to go!"

Katashi shook his head. It was no use. He wasn't able to

move on his own.

Stan lay motionless. Robotman paced around the fallen kaiju. There was no sign of life.

Robotman stepped closer. The mecha-protector had to confirm that Stan was indeed dead.

But Stan was not.

The kaiju moved swiftly. Its boney scythe swung through the air and pierced Robotman's foot. Sparks flew as metal ripped away from the mech.

Robotman tore apart from its trapped foot. The robot limped back several steps. Stan sat up. Its head turned toward Robotman.

The mech adjusted its weight. It could no longer stand properly on its feet with its right foot damaged as it was.

Stan stood back up. It did not stop this time. It marched toward Robotman with unrelenting determination.

"What are we going to do?" Masaki asked Katashi from outside the car. "We need to get you moved out of the driver seat."

"Just go without me," said Katashi. "Run!"

"I said I wasn't going to leave you," said Masaki.

"You have to," said Katashi. "For real this time. You have to leave me here."

"No," said Masaki. She looked inside the car for anything that would help. Then she had an idea. She reached through the broken window and grabbed the car's radio intercom.

"Hello!" she called out. "Hello! My name is Ota Masaki. I'm trapped in the tunnel with Detective Ishida Katashi. We need your help. The kaiju is after us!"

"It's no use," said Katashi. "The damn thing is probably broken."

"No, they'll hear us," said Masaki confidently.

"Just go!" ordered Katashi.

Then the sound of salvation crackled through the radio speakers.

"Ota Masaki this is Captain Hashimoto Akane," was said through the radio. "We are homing in on your position. Robotman has the kaiju at bay. K.A.R.R.D. is preparing the area."

"Can you help us?!" Masaki yelled into the intercom.

Katashi grumbled. Then he grabbed the mic from Masaki's hands.

"This is Detective Katashi," he said. "What's the situation? Is there a rescue on the way?"

"K.A.R.R.D. is seeing to the matter," said Hashimoto. "Robotman just has to weaken the kaiju and then K.A.R.R.D. will trigger a trap. There is a poison gas wall forming some blocks away in the Tsukiji District. Once the kaiju is inside the kill zone it will fall. I suggest you two sit tight. We will be with you when Robotman defeats the kaiju."

"Sit tight?!" Katashi hollered. "We're under attack. Stan wants us. He is going after us. We need to get out of here."

Robotman changed tactics. Its eyes lit up for its Robot Flash. Two beams shot out of Robotman's eyes and hit Stan. The energy enveloped the kaiju. Suddenly, Stan was immobile.

Stan struggled to break free from Robotman's hold. Its body twitched and convulsed against the radiating power of Robotman's Robot Flash. Robotman held its guard, hands firmly at its hips.

With the kaiju at bay, Robotman used the time to reroute power through its body. It needed to regroup if it was going to combat Stan any further.

Stan was weak in Robotman's hold. Its arms were pinned down to its side. Robotman circled its stunned target, favoring its foot.

Stan pushed harder against the Robot Flash. The power radiating from Robotman wafted in the air. Stan struggled to break free.

Sensing the urgency, Robotman rushed forward. Stan broke free from the energy hold. The kaiju's arms swung wide to strike.

Robotman slipped in first. It jumped up into the air. A knee struck Stan in the ribcage as Robotman went high. Then its metallic fist came crashing down.

Punch!

Punch!

Punch!

A flurry of punches hit Stan square in the jaw.

Robotman landed back on the ground as Stan collapsed back into the rubble.

A square block of Tokyo was destroyed. Buildings were now a pile of rocks all around Stan and Robotman. Dust polluted the air. It would be unknown how many lives were lost in the fight between the two behemoths.

"Stan is down again," said Masaki, watching the fight from the edge of the tunnel.

Katashi readjusted in the driver's seat of the car. He could only move a couple of inches at a time. His legs were dead weight. The best he could do was shove his legs over as he shifted the rest of his body.

"Will the gas kill it?" Masaki asked.

"Yes," said Katashi. "And anything else inside the kill zone. If people haven't evacuated they're all dead."

"Will it reach us here?" Masaki wondered.

"No," said Katashi. "They would have warned us. Robotman will get Stan into place. We just have to pray it happens before the tunnel collapses. They could destroy the whole city in this fight. Won't have to worry about gas at that point."

"So they're not coming?" asked Masaki.

"Not for us," said Katashi. "We're on our own. Nobody is looking out for you, kid. That's the truth."

Masaki sighed.

Only she could look out for herself now.

Robotman stood tall in the debris. It waited again for Stan to get back up. The smoke and dust were thick at its feet. Stan was lost to the clutter. There was no telling if the kaiju was moving.

The mech waited. The silence in the city was deafening.

Robotman kicked into the smoke.

Stan was gone.

Robotman kicked several more times, moving smoke in the vain effort to find Stan.

Then a scythe reached out from the smoke behind Robotman.

The blade cut through the metal armor of the mech and came out the other side along the thigh. Robotman was trapped.

Stan climbed up to its feet. The kaiju towered over Robotman.

Stan's other hand reached out. It wrapped its arm around Robotman's head, allowing the blade of its boney scythe to brace up against Robotman's neck.

Robotman struggled to break free. Its hands latched on to Stan's arms, trying to break the kaiju's powerful hold. Stan released the scythe in Robotman's thigh. The kaiju lifted Robotman into the air. The mech's legs kicked wildly.

More pressure went around Robotman's head. Metal groaned as Stan squeezed.

Robotman's eyes cracked. The energy of the Robot Flash

fizzled out as Stan refused to relinquish the hold.

Stan roared in certain victory.

Robotman's kicks grew weak. The mech was losing power. Sparks died away. Its hands fell from Stan's skull crushing grip.

The sound of metal cracking boomed across Tokyo. Robotman's head imploded.

Stan roared again as Robotman's body went limp.

The mecha-protector of Asia was defeated.

Stan tossed the giant robot off to the side. The metal carcass crashed into several buildings. Tokyo's destructions became the burial ground for their giant hero.

Stan paused for a moment, examining its latest work.

Down below in the tunnel, Masaki's heart sank. Robotman was their last hope. What could stop Stan now?

Stan shifted. The kaiju turned its attention back to the tunnel.

Nobody was going to save Masaki.

She stared at the approaching Stan.

Nobody was going to save Masaki.

She was going to save herself.

Chapter 20

Now, unopposed, Stan concentrated its full strength on the tunnel at its feet. The kaiju slammed its scythes into the top of the tunnel with full force. The repeated blows were enough to chip away at the tunnel. Larger chunks of the ceiling collapsed, revealing the interior.

Sunlight shinned into the tunnel. Masaki looked up from the street. Stan was visible through the ceiling of the tunnel. The towering monster would not relent. Another blow shook the tunnel and dropped Masaki to her knees. It was only a matter of time before Stan fully broke through the tunnel's structure.

Masaki raced back to Katashi in the car. He was halfway off the driver's seat. He bit back the pain that every shift to the left caused him.

"Move!" Masaki yelled as she opened the driver side door. She put all of her weight into her shoulder and shoved Katashi further off of the driver's seat.

He screamed, releasing all of his pain and frustration in one go. His legs bent awkwardly as the upper half of his body slammed into the passenger side window.

Masaki scooped up Katashi's legs and dropped them on the

other side of the car, nearly straightening Katashi in the passenger seat. Sweat dripped down his face as he breathed a sigh of relief.

"What are you doing?" Katashi asked. "We can't go out there. Stan is waiting for us."

"We can't wait here," said Masaki. "And Robotman was destroyed."

Katashi groaned. He was out of options.

"Where is the K.A.R.R.D. trap?" Masaki asked.

"What?!" Katashi questioned.

"Stan is after us," said Masaki. "We can take him to the trap."

Katashi shook his head. The idea was insane. But he was worried that Masaki was also right.

"The gas will kill us," said Katashi.

"We can drive right through it," assured Masaki.

The street rumbled from another blow of Stan's offense. A large slab of concrete crashed onto the pavement near the car. Masaki screamed. She hit the gas out of instinct. The car shot forward, nearly careening into one of the dozens of abandoned cars in the tunnel.

"Watch it!" Katashi yelled once Masaki had slammed on the brakes.

Another piece of the ceiling collapsed onto the street. Stan was more visible than ever. And its next strike was even worse.

A scythe dived straight into the tunnel through one of the openings in the roof. The boney blade of Stan pierced the street several meters away from Masaki and Katashi. Then the scythe ripped away at the ceiling as Stan recoiled its hand.

"We have to go!" Masaki yelled. She put her foot down on the pedal once again this time with more control over the steering.

The car shot off down the tunnel. Masaki spun wildly through the congested street, scraping the car against the concrete wall and littered debris.

"The trap is at the Tsukiji district," Katashi said. "When you get past Stan, drive as fast as you can. I'll tell you when to turn."

The entrance of the tunnel was nearing. Stan's feet were like tree trunks. Masaki drifted toward the left to avoid the obstacle.

Stan raised both its arms into the air. The roof of the tunnel was nearly gone. One more blow would destroy what was left of its frame.

Then the car shot out of the tunnel. Stan watched as it buzzed past its feet and continued down the rubble street.

The road was bumpy and uneven. The fight between Stan and Robotman had nearly destroyed the entire area. Masaki and Katashi bounced up and down in their seats as the car pushed on. Katashi winced every time his legs knocked against the side of the car.

Stan turned around. Its attention was no longer on the tunnel. The kaiju could sense its prey in the car racing away.

Each ease of step brought Stan closer to the car. It was damaged and the path through the rubble was only making it worse. It was not a matter of if, but when Stan could catch up with them.

Masaki struggled to keep the car from veering off. The wheel vibrated in her hand violently. Stan was in her rear-view mirror.

"Turn here!" Katashi ordered.

The turn was tight. Masaki closed her eyes and forced the car to make a right turn. The tires squealed. For a moment, the left side tires left the ground. Katashi could feel the weightlessness in his stomach. Then they came crashing down and the car sped forward onto the new street.

Stan did not miss a step. The kaiju continued its pursuit. The turn allowed Stan to get closer. The monster was now within range to strike out with its scythes.

The car struggled to gain speed. Masaki pressed down on the gas pedal but was only given the roaring displeasure of the engine. Masaki looked back. Only Stan's legs were visible in the rear-view mirror. He was getting closer.

"What do you think you are doing?" came the familiar voice of Captain Hashimoto over the radio.

Katashi fumbled for the intercom. It bounced around in his hand several times before he was able to gain control.

"We're bringing Stan to you," he replied.

"Turn away," said Hashimoto. "If you are caught in the gas trap you will all be killed."

"Too late," said Katashi. "Get ready. Stan is on his way."

"Detective Katashi," reiterated Hashimoto. "Turn around now. We will get Stan another way. Air support is nearby."

"Stan is after us!" Katashi yelled into the intercom. "Air supports, tanks, none of that is going to help us right now. We are on the run, and we are running to you. Get ready!"

Then he threw the intercom out of his hand. There was nothing left to argue about. The plan was set.

Stan lunged forward. Its right scythe hand slammed into the street ahead of the car. Masaki screamed and turned the wheel violently, skidding the car away from the giant scythe. Then Stan's second scythe came crashing down. This time the scythe scraped against the car.

The driver side door ripped away.

The sudden collision and rush of wind caught Masaki off guard. She swerved the car back and forth struggling to regain control.

"We're almost there," said Katashi. "Turn left here!"

Masaki did as she was instructed. The car took a wide turn onto another street. Stan used the chance to step closer, nearly overtaking the car completely.

Masaki looked up from her doorless side of the car. She was directly underneath the kaiju.

Up ahead, it was a straight shot. Military waited down the street. Bolt tanks were positioned along the sidewalks. Rocket tanks hung out in the back, ready to fire at their kaiju target.

K.A.R.R.D.'s air strike was the first to attack. Jets flew overhead, firing missiles at Stan. The attack halted Stan in its tracks allowing Masaki and Katashi to regain some distance from the kaiju.

Stan roared. Its tentacle mouth danced in the air.

Energy beams and rockets struck Stan. Explosions reigned down around the kaiju. Stan cried out in defiance.

Then the kaiju advanced further. K.A.R.R.D.'s initial attack did little damage to the monster.

Katashi turned his head with much pain to look out the back window of the car. Stan was not stopping.

Masaki drove past the first row of Bolt Tanks. Their electrical beams fired out at Stan, lighting up the afternoon sky.

Stan dismissed the attacks from the street, focusing only on Masaki and Katashi in the car. The energy strikes prodded and burned the kaiju, but they did not stop the monster.

"Stan has entered the kill zone," announced Captain Hashimoto over the radio. "Get out now."

Masaki gritted her teeth. She pushed down harder on the gas pedal hoping the car would understand her demand to go faster.

Canisters shot into the air. They rained down on the street, releasing yellowish brown gas.

Masaki coughed. There was no protection from the deadly gas. Their car was nearly destroyed. Her car door was gone. The gas rolled into the interior with ease.

At first her skin itched. Then it turned into a burning sensation. Tears welled up in her eyes, preventing her from seeing the road clearly.

The gas began to rise. The smoke filled the sky surrounding Stan.

The kaiju swung its scythes wildly, trying to fend off the gas attack. The deadly gas acted the same for kaiju as it did for humans. Stan's skin began to turn red from the destructive heat. Soon the gas would eat away at the kaiju and anything else organic that was within range.

Unable to fend off the gas attack, Stan dropped to a knee, falling deeper into the poisoned air.

Masaki clawed at her arms and her cheeks. Her whole body tingled with pins and needles. She could feel her energy draining. Katashi's body was already deteriorating. Flakes of skin brushed off his face from the wind.

The air was thick with the deadly gas, but Masaki could see clearer skies not far ahead. They were almost out of the kill zone.

"Hang on," she said to Katashi. "We're almost there."

"You're doing great," said Katashi.

Then Stan's scythe reached out from the poison gas.

Masaki did not see it coming. The boney blade split the back of the car into two, sending it into a tailspin.

Debris flung into the air. The back tires evaporated into dust.

The passengers of the car slammed headfirst into the dashboard.

The car came to its final stop. Still several meters inside of K.A.R.R.D.'s kill zone.

Stan shuffled somewhere in the dense smoke. Only its rumbles could be heard.

Masaki shifted in the car seat. Her skin burned, but she paid no attention to that anymore. She looked over at Katashi. The older detective was breathing heavily. His eyes were distant.

"We have to go," said Masaki.

Katashi coughed. He shook his head.

Masaki reached out for him, but Katashi brushed her arms out of the way.

"Go!" Katashi yelled. "Get out of here."

"What about you?" Masaki asked.

Katashi shook his head again. "This is it. I'm not making it out of here. No way."

"I can't leave you," said Masaki.

"You have to," said Katashi. "I'll buy you some time."

"How?"

"Just go!" Katashi yelled. He leaned over, screaming in pain while doing so, and shoved Masaki out of the car.

Masaki rolled across the pavement. Even the ground was hot from the smoke contamination. She took in a deep breath, only to regret it. A coughing fit took over.

Another rumble came from deeper in the smoke. Stan was still in there. Alive.

Masaki forced herself to her feet. One step at a time she pushed on, getting ever so closer to fresh air.

Stan's scythe slammed into the street. Masaki stopped. Then the other scythe crashed down. Masaki knelt down but kept moving forward. Just as fast as the scythes appeared they were pulled away. Stan could not see her. The kaiju was lashing out wildly.

The scythes came crashing down again. Masaki ran faster. Fear turned into adrenaline. She was almost clear. The car disappeared in the smoke behind her.

Katashi leaned against the car door. His body twisted in an unnatural position.

The street shook as Stan crawled closer to Katashi and the car.

Stan emerged from the smoke. Its giant head dwarfing the car Katashi was in. Skin peeled away from the kaiju revealing muscle and bone. Drips of blood and goo piled onto the street.

The kaiju looked down at the old man. Its head tilted; almost disappointed Masaki was not with him.

Stan screamed. Its mouth tentacles reached out and enveloped the car.

Katashi smiled.

He hadn't retreated. He had saved the little girl this time.

Stan shot forward. The kaiju's body crushed the car with Katashi inside.

And then there was one.

Masaki was slowing down. The deadly smoke was becoming too much.

The street rumbled beneath her. Stan was close by.

But it wasn't Stan.

Masaki looked up. Tanks rolled into the edge of the smoke screen.

Relief washed over her. Almost instantly, her body dropped.

Soldiers rushed forward. They grabbed hold of Masaki and pulled her farther away from the smoke. An O2 mask was thrown around her face. She breathed in deeply like she had never had fresh air before.

She was free.

She had made it.

But Stan had other plans.

The kaiju thrust out of the smoke. Its scythes slammed down into the street, crushing several soldiers that were in the way.

The group protecting Masaki fell to the ground.

The young woman froze.

Stan dragged itself forward. It stared down Masaki.

Masaki stared back at the grotesque kaiju Stan had become.

Hate had fueled the monster. No longer would Stan be disregarded.

But Masaki no longer had any hate. She no longer feared Stan. She no longer feared the world that awaited her.

Stan let out one last roar before death came for the vile soul once more.

The kaiju's body slumped to the ground. Its scythes fell over.

Silence eased the tension.

Masaki did not move. She stared at Stan.

The monster was dead.

Chapter 21

Reconstruction was already beginning in sporadic areas of Tokyo. The path of destruction across the city would eventually just be a memory. The deadly smoke had evaporated. Stan's body was left a pile of mush when it was all said and done. All that was left was the rubble to clean up.

Masaki sat alone in the back of a police car. The running lights of the sirens kept her focused in the now. She dared not think about the events that had just happened or what was going to happen in the future.

Captain Hashimoto approached her. Masaki shrugged. She readjusted the blanket that was around her shoulders. Her lungs still hurt but she was able to talk.

"How are you feeling?" asked Hashimoto.

"Okay," said Masaki.

"Is there anybody we can call for you?"

Masaki hesitated.

"Family?" Captain Hashimoto pushed.

"No," said Masaki. "They're gone."

"Do you have some place to go?" Hashimoto asked. "Should I call child services?"

"No," said Masaki. She looked straight at the K.A.R.R.D.

commander. “I'm an adult. I'll be fine.”

Captain Hashimoto nodded her head. “Okay. Sit tight. We'll have somebody check on you shortly. Then we'll get you settled for the night. K.A.R.R.D. will take care of you.”

Masaki nodded. This was the world that awaited her now, one where she knew her responsibility and her value.

This was her Coming of Age Day.

Message from the Author

Hi,

Thank you for reading my book. Whether you bought it directly from me or on-line I really appreciate it. Every customer makes me believe that maybe I know what I'm doing and I'm heading in the right direction with my dreams.

I hope you liked it. I hope you found the excitement that I have when I'm not only writing the book but also discovering the story along the way.

If you wish to continue to support me then please be sure to leave a review. The most helpful place is Amazon where my books are sold. Every review counts. (Even if you hated it, and somehow you've made it to the end here to read this letter).

I have links on my website, danegkroll.com, or you can use a QR Reader and scan the box down below to take you directly to my Amazon Author Page.

Frankly, I'm probably going to be writing until I'm dead. But if you want books out faster then show your support and leave a review. Also, find my Facebook page and let me know as well. You can also look at mediocre pictures of my cat.

Thanks again for spending your time with my adventures. I hope you come back for more.

Dane G. Kroll

www.ingramcontent.com/pod-product-compliance
Lightning Source LLC
LaVergne TN
LVHW031343150826
845673LV00009B/2847

9798832406855